SPECIAL MESSAGE TO READERS

This book is published under the auspices of
THE ULVERSCROFT FOUNDATION
(registered charity No. 264873 UK)

Established in 1972 to provide funds for research, diagnosis and treatment of eye diseases. Examples of contributions made are: —

A new Children's Assessment Unit at Moorfield's Hospital, London.

•

Twin operating theatres at the Western Ophthalmic Hospital, London.

•

A Chair of Ophthalmology at the University of Leicester.

•

The establishment of a Royal Australian College of Ophthalmologists "Fellowship".

You can help further the work of the Foundation by making a donation or leaving a legacy. Every contribution, no matter how small, is received with gratitude. Please write for details to:

THE ULVERSCROFT FOUNDATION,
The Green, Bradgate Road, Anstey,
Leicester LE7 7FU, England.
Telephone: (0116) 236 4325

In Australia write to:
THE ULVERSCROFT FOUNDATION,
c/o The Royal Australian College of
Ophthalmologists,
27, Commonwealth Street, Sydney,
N.S.W. 2010.

BRAND: HARDCASE

When Ben Wyatt and his gang hold up the bank in Adobe, Arizona, Wyatt is captured as they flee the scene. Sheriff Willard Beal and a deputy had been gunned down in the raid and the only man left to guard the brutal bank robber is the remaining deputy, young Rick Lander. Judge Rice is summoned and he asks Jason Brand, an ex-U.S. Marshal, to take up the silver star. Wyatt is in the cells, his men close by, and Brand is the only man to get Adobe out of real trouble . . .

Books by Neil Hunter
in the Linford Western Library:

BODIE:
TRACKDOWN
BLOODY BOUNTY
HIGH HELL
THE KILLING TRAIL
HANGTOWN
THE DAY OF THE SAVAGE

BRAND:
GUN FOR HIRE

NEIL HUNTER

BRAND: HARDCASE

Complete and Unabridged

LINFORD
Leicester

First Linford Edition
published 1997

British Library CIP Data

Hunter, Neil
   Brand: hardcase.—Large print ed.—
Linford western library
   1. English fiction—20th century
   2. Large type books
   I. Title
   823.9′14 [F]

   ISBN 0–7089–5041–8

Published by
F. A. Thorpe (Publishing) Ltd.
Anstey, Leicestershire

Set by Words & Graphics Ltd.
Anstey, Leicestershire
Printed and bound in Great Britain by
T. J. Press (Padstow) Ltd., Padstow, Cornwall

This book is printed on acid-free paper

1

THE town was called Adobe. It had been around for almost twenty-five years, basing its existence and prosperity on the surrounding cattle country. The wild and harsh Arizona territory might not have seemed a hospitable host to any form of life, but despite the heat, the scant vegetation and the often acute shortage of water, the herds of cattle that roamed the ranges thrived and multiplied. As the outlying ranches grew so did Adobe, beginning as nothing more than a trading post and slowly developing. The demands of the cowhands from the various ranches soon added saloons and gambling houses, and early on a couple of brothels. Then someone built a livery stable, followed by a barber shop. Next a stage began to call. The owners of the line built a depot. With the arrival of more people came the need for eating houses, even a hotel. In 1865, the year of the town's 10th anniversary, Adobe's bank opened for business. 1873 saw the opening of a Wells and Fargo Stage, Freight and Security office. Wells and Fargo also bought out the local stageline and established a fully operational swing-station, building corrals and a second livery stable. By the mid-80's Adobe was a well established town. It had its own resident Judge, a stone courthouse and jail, and a fulltime lawman.

His name was Willard Beal. He was thirty-five years old. A tall, broad shouldered man who always wore a black suit and a white shirt. Beal kept the law in Adobe with a firm hand. He had a reputation for being hard but fair. When it came to using his gun he had a simple rule; if a man comes at you with a gun in his hand treat him like a potential killer and act accordingly. More than one

2

self-styled fast gun had tried to add Willard Beal's name to his list of kills. They had all failed and were buried in Adobe's cemetery.

Despite his past record, and his ability to handle situations, Beal was still a man at the end of the day. He was as mortal as the next and a bullet was liable to injure him just the same. Beal found this out one day in mid-summer. It would be the first time he ever stopped a bullet. It also turned out to be the last time . . .

It began like any other day in Adobe. Like countless days in the past. But before this particular one was over Adobe was to know violence and terror — and there would be fresh graves in the cemetery.

Beal and his deputies had completed their morning routine. It was close on ten. The town was simmering beneath a blazing sun. By noon the temperature would be even higher. The town lay on a wide, near flat plain, with the foothills of the Gila Bend Mountains

3

to the north. The heat, dropping out of a cloudless sky, was caught by the hard surface of the land and radiated back. Adobe sweltered slowly and went about its business. The townspeople had learned long ago that the only way to exist in this climate was by taking matters at a steady pace. Only fools and madmen rushed about.

Beal was taking a slow walk back to his office for coffee when he heard the distant cry go up.

"Fire! Fire at Clover's livery!"

Beal turned on his heel, glancing back along the street. He saw the smoke just beginning to drift out over the rooftops at the far end of town. As he turned to retrace his steps he caught sight of his two deputies.

"George, get on over to Hardy's place and see he gets that fire wagon out fast!"

Seeing his deputy hoof it across to Vern Hardy's blacksmith shop, Beal carried on towards the source of the fire. The town was coming to life around him. People were crowding the boardwalks, craning their necks to get a better look. Others were heading down to the livery. As Beal neared the place he saw flames leaping out of the livery's open doors. The shrill scream of frightened horses filled the air.

As he drew level with the alley running up the side of the stable Beal saw movement. He paused and saw a man's stooped figure by the wall. The man was leaning against the side of the stable, head down, arms drawn round his body. He looked as if he might be hurt. *Maybe he's been inside the stable*, Beal thought. He moved towards the man.

"Hey, you hurt, fella?" he asked.

The man responded to Beal's question. But not the way the lawman had expected. And a split-second before that response Beal got a feeling something wasn't right about the situation. Instinct took over and Beal reached for his gun.

He didn't make it.

The stooped figure suddenly straightened up. There was a cocked .45 calibre Colt in his right hand, and the muzzle was aimed at Beal. The barrel was only inches from Beal's shirt. The lawman felt fear claw at his gut when he saw the gun. He caught a brief glimpse of the man's face grinning at him.

"Ever been had, Marshal?"

The Colt went off with a hard sound. Beal was slammed across the alley by the impact of the heavy bullet. He hit the far wall, his body already reacting to the stunning force of the bullet that had torn its way through his chest and out between his shoulders, taking part of one lung with it. There was a pulpy hole in his back where the projectile had emerged. As Beal slumped against the wall the Colt fired a second time, this bullet adding to the damage of the first. Beal flopped loosely in the dirt a terrible weakness sweeping over him. Sound filled his ears and he found it hard to breathe. The taste of blood filled his mouth. Pain began to wash over him, increasing rapidly. He wished it would stop. When it did he slid into the enveloping blackness gratefully, unaware that he was dying. By the time he was found it was too late to do anything but think about burying him.

★ ★ ★

With the majority of the town down at Clover's livery the staff of Adobe's bank found they were without customers. That was until six armed men forced their way into the bank, closing and locking the doors behind them.

"Nobody moves, nobody gets hurt!"

The order was given by a tall, heavy-built man in his late thirties. He was darkhaired, with pale blue eyes, and he might have been handsome if it hadn't been for the livid scar running down the left side of his face.

Frank Pearson, one of the tellers,

took one look at the scar and recognised the man who owned it.

"It's Ben Wyatt," he exclaimed to no one in particular.

Wyatt turned in Pearson's direction. His tanned face, unshaven and gaunt, was made to look almost evil because of that long dead-white scar running from temple to jawline.

"Know me, do you, boy?" he asked, his tone friendly.

"Who doesn't?" Pearson grinned in sudden bravado.

Wyatt returned the grin. He was still grinning as he shot the young teller. Pearson crashed to the floor with two bullets in his chest and blood all over his suit.

"Now the rest of you tend your business," Wyatt demanded harshly. "All you have to do is hand out the money. We'll just collect it."

Close to Wyatt stood his younger brother, Al. If Ben Wyatt was known for his brutality, his younger brother was renowned for his instability. There were many who said that Al Wyatt was crazy. It might have been true. He was certainly abnormal. Al had a strange, sinister quality to his character that put the rest of the Wyatt bunch on their guard when he was about. Al was mistrusted by them all. They only tolerated him because he was Ben's brother, and the bunch was loyal to Ben Wyatt. They were aware that Ben always sided with his younger brother, granting him every whim. No one could explain why Ben had this unswerving devotion for his brother, because there were even times when Al would turn on Ben too, cursing and raging at him until his mood ebbed away. Yet each time this happened Ben would take all without a murmer.

"Hey, Ben, you sure straightened him out," Al said, giggling to himself. He peered down at Pearson's prone figure. Then a shot rang out. "He was still wriggling, Ben. He ain't any more."

One of the young female tellers

began to scream. Ben Wyatt strode over to her. Without warning he struck her across the face with the barrel of his gun. The screaming ceased as the girl fell back against the counter, clutching a slim white hand to her face. Blood began to trickle through her fingers, dripping on to the crisp starched blouse she was wearing.

"Anybody else even looks the wrong way," Ben Wyatt yelled, "and I'll drop the whole damn lot of you! Now get those bags filled."

There was no more trouble. The tellers fell to stuffing the saddlebags provided with every banknote they could find. While this went on Ben Wyatt paced the floor. He was feeling restless. Uneasy. Being cooped up inside the bank didn't settle well with him. He had a thing about confining spaces. Deep inside he was getting a feeling something wasn't right. He didn't know why he was feeling that way — but it was growing stronger with each passing second, and his instincts were telling him to get the hell out of Adobe.

And fast.

"Ben. We're set!"

Jake Sutter had been with Wyatt for a long time. Sutter, a tall, lean grey-eyed Texan had built his reputation as a cold, deadly killer who could do things with his bone-handled Colt most others said was impossible. The ones who could confirm his skill were all dead. Now he carried a pair of bulging saddlebags over his shoulder.

"You look like a man with a bad case of the runs, Ben."

His tone was light, but concerned. He knew Ben Wyatt well — and could recognise when the man was worried about something.

"Sooner we get out of this town the better I'll like it, Jake." Wyatt stared out at their tethered horses. "Hell! It's starting to fall apart."

He crossed to the door and yanked it open.

"Let's go, boys," he yelled, stepping

out on to the boardwalk, his gun up and ready.

The rest of the bunch filed from the bank. For a moment they paused, staring. The town lay oddly silent and deserted. It was quiet.

Too quiet.

Al Wyatt's shrill voice split the silence.

"Hey, Ben, we went and scared the damn town away!"

"Shut up, you sorry excuse for an asshole," Jake Sutter said tautly. He was developing the same feeling Ben Wyatt had admitted to. The job *was* going wrong. And they were right in the middle of a hostile town.

Al, his face stiff with anger, rounded on Sutter. "Ben," he whined, "you hear what he . . . "

"Keep quiet, Al," Ben snapped.

The first shot came then. Fired from across the street by someone too nervous to hold back any longer. The bullet whacked the bank's stone facing and howled off into the blue.

"Throw down your weapons! There's no way out!"

The command reached the outlaws clearly, coming from the shadows of an alley across from the bank.

Jake Sutter heard Ben Wyatt's sharp hiss of anger.

"Ben, you feel like quitting?" he asked.

"Oh sure," Wyatt remarked dryly. Then he yelled out: "Head out, boys, and scatter! Every man for himself!"

They broke away from the bank frontage, guns up and firing. Return fire came from the concealed men across the street. The air was split by the multiple explosions. Bullets crisscrossed the street. They gouged the dirt. Ripped splinters from the boardwalk and whacked the stone wall of the bank. Some struck the big, gilded main window, shattering it.

In the confusion of those first seconds Ben Wyatt saw one of his men go down, then a second, bodies twisting and spouting blood. The rain of bullets tore them to bloody rags. There was no time to stop and help.

The tethered horses were milling about in panic, jostling each other. The noise and the yelling, maybe even the smell of blood was adding to their agitation.

Wyatt grabbed the reins of his own horse. Out the corner of his eye he saw Al already in his saddle, firing wildly in all directions. Next to him was Sutter. The tall Texan, cool as ever, seemed oblivious to the gunfire as he dropped his loaded saddlebags over his saddle. Dragging himself aboard his own mount Ben Wyatt was aware of the sick feeling in his stomach again, and cursed his own weakness. He pulled the horse's head round and sent it along the street, laying low across its neck.

There seemed to be a hundred guns firing at them from all directions. The air was thick with flying lead.

Ben Wyatt thundered down the dusty street. He could hear horses close by.

The thud of hooves mingled with the steady crash of gunfire.

What a godawful mess!

His horse took a bullet. A spray of hot blood arced up as the stricken animal screamed in agony. Wyatt felt it going down and he kicked his feet free of the stirrups, flinging himself clear. He hit hard, his face and shoulder scraping along in the gritty dust. Stunned by the fall he lay helpless, dust clogging his eyes and throat.

He knew he had to get up. They would be on him in seconds if he stayed where he was. He raised his head. Blood was spilling from his torn chin. Wyatt got his hands under him, shoving off the ground. He picked up the sound of pounding boots behind him somewhere and clawed for his gun. His holster was empty, then he remembered he had been holding the gun when his horse fell. The horse! His rifle . . . in the scabbard . . .

"Touch it and you're dead!"

Ben Wyatt froze, his fingers inches

from the rifle's stock. The tone of the voice was enough to convince him not to try for the rifle. With his anger mounting Wyatt straightened up, his hands held well away from his body. He turned and found himself face to face with a slim, fairhaired young man wearing a Deputy badge on his shirt. There was a rifle in his hands, aimed at Wyatt's chest.

"Boy, you keep a tight hold of that piece, 'cause if I see it shake just once I'll take it and shove it up your ass barrel-end first."

A second man joined the deputy. He was thin and unshaven, carrying a single- barrel shotgun. "Talks big, don't he, Rick?"

"He won't when Judge Rice puts a rope 'round his neck," Rick said.

"I'll tell you something, boy," Wyatt said, relaxing a little. "I been close to a noose a number of times, and I'm still here. So don't crow too loud. I ain't dead yet."

The skinny man laughed. "If you

think your gang's going to come and get you, Wyatt, don't hold your breath. They're clear out of town and still going. Be the last we'll see of them."

Ben Wyatt didn't say a word. He wouldn't have expected his men to do anything else under the circumstances. They would ride all right. Just far enough to lose any pursuit, and once they were safe Jake Sutter would hole them up while he figured out a rescue plan. The tall Texan had a smart head on his shoulders and he knew how to use it.

The shooting had died down now. The street was suddenly alive with people, most of whom had come to stare at Ben Wyatt. This would be a day to remember. It would become part of Adobe's history. The day Ben Wyatt's gang raided the bank and killed Willard Beal and one of the tellers. What would be remembered even longer would be the capture of Wyatt himself. One of the Southwest's worst outlaws. The man the law had been after for years. And now Adobe had him. Their prisoner. To be tried and hanged and buried in Adobe.

Rick, the young deputy, prodded Wyatt with his rifle.

"Jail's behind you. Let's go. And walk easy, 'cause I got every reason in the world to blow you apart."

Wyatt smiled coldly at him. "After all I done for you, boy? Just no gratitude left in the world. Hell, didn't I arrange for the marshal to get killed for you? Left the way clear so you can step into his job?"

"*Bastard!*" The word exploded from Rick's mouth. He lashed out with the rifle and clouted Wyatt across the side of the head, driving him to his knees.

Rick turned to the skinny man. "Charley, go down to Judge Rice's and ask him to step over to the jail."

Charley nodded and hurried away.

"On your feet, Wyatt, and move."

Ben Wyatt stood up, swaying a little. He raised his head to stare at Rick. There was pure hate in his eyes. Blood was running down his battered face, dripping onto his dirty shirt. Sweat gleamed on his skin and in that moment he seemed more animal than man.

Despite the fact that he was holding a loaded gun on the outlaw, Rick had a moment of extreme unease. He realised that having Ben Wyatt locked away in a cell wasn't going to bring an end to this affair. The man was going to bring trouble to Adobe. And it was going to reach out and touch a lot of people.

2

THE noise and shooting had woken him from a restless sleep.

Jason Brand sat up, groaning in disgust. His head ached and his mouth tasted foul. He swung his legs off the low cot and stood up, feeling the stone floor of the cell move under his feet. He braced a hand against the cell wall until the feeling passed.

Too much bad whisky and not enough food.

He focussed on the commotion outside. All hell seemed to have broken loose. Men were shouting. Horses shrilling. And it sounded like every gun in Adobe was being fired off at the same time. Brand turned across the cell, searching for the pail of drinking water. Finding it he dipped in the ladle and drank deeply. The water

20

sluiced down his throat and hit his stomach like a lead ball. He scrubbed a hand across his face, feeling the thick stubble. *Christ, what a state to be in.* No wonder Judge Rice had given him fourteen days to get straightened out. He wondered wryly whether fourteen days was long enough.

He'd been in a drunken haze for longer than he could clearly recall. He wasn't even sure how long he'd been in Adobe. A week — two? Most of it had been spent down in shacktown. Brand stumbled back to the cot and sat down with his head in his hands, wishing all the racket outside would cease.

He vaguely remembered collecting his 10,000 dollars from Morgan Dorsey, fixing himself up with a horse and fresh gear, and riding off to find a Mexican girl called Sarita. The problem was he never made it. He had been warned to rest up by the doctor back in Concho, but ignored the advice. He had badly bruised ribs and a whole mess of gashes and cuts, plus a couple of deep bullet gouges. But he had wanted to get clear of the Dorsey affair, clear it from his mind and move on. So he'd saddled up and ridden out. Two days later he was burning with fever, out of his head, hardly knowing who he was. He had drifted down to the border and found himself a room in a fly-blown hotel in some forgotten little settlement. He'd stayed there for almost two weeks, drinking some evil local *pulque* because there was nothing else available. The drink had been to wash away the taste of the food, which had a distinctly odd tang under the heavy spicing. The only consolation was that the hotel's Mexican owner had a daughter, who was both young, pretty and extremely accommodating. She had the kind of figure that even Brand, in his feverish state, could appreciate. He lost track of the hours she spent with him in the hotel's hot, airless room, her naked brown body glistening with sweat as she wriggled and thrust beneath him, encircling him with her supple, powerful thighs.

Yet even those endless days and nights were not enough to empty his mind, and he had left the settlement still angry and sickened by the actions of the people he'd been involved with. People like Ramon Huerta. Carla Dorsey. Saul Hussler. They had dreamed up a plan and had carried it through without thought or conscience for the outcome. It was the cold, calculating way they had worked that had soured Brand. He knew he should have been immune to it now. But there were still times when it reached him, leaving him disgusted and bitter by the evil people practised.

Brand had reached Adobe by way of Tombstone. While stopping over in Tombstone he had lost a large chunk of his 10,000 at the poker tables. By the time he reached Adobe he had a little over 3,000 left. The gambling tables of Adobe took another large bite out of what remained. Women and whisky finished off the rest. On the day he got into the fight with a pair of quarrelsome cowhands he was down to his last 200 dollars. He'd been edgy all that day and the goading from the cowhands pushed him over the edge. Brand took a beating himself, considering it worth it because of the satisfaction he got from laying out the belligerent cowhands. The fight was ended with the appearance of Willard Beal, Adobe's Marshal. Beal had been keeping an eye on the man he'd known as a US Marshal, and that was how Brand found himself before Judge Caleb Rice. He knew the Judge, like he knew Beal, through his former profession. Rice had listened to Beal's evidence and without hesitation had sentenced Brand to fourteen days in Adobe's jail.

Brand had been in his cell for three days now. It was beginning to tell on him. With every passing hour the cell got smaller. He didn't relish the thought of another eleven days behind bars. He had just drifted off into a shallow sleep when the crackle of gunfire woke him.

He didn't bother to lie down again. Just sat on the edge of the cot and waited for the shooting to stop. When it did the silence became oppressive. Brand became curious as to what had been going on.

The jail's outer door opened. Boots clattered across the office's wooden floor. Voices rose and fell. Then the door leading to the cell area swung open and a man moved reluctantly into the passage.

Brand recognised him instantly.

It was Ben Wyatt.

The face was well known to Jason Brand. He had seen it glaring down at him from hundreds of 'Wanted' dodgers all across the southwest. Wyatt and his bunch had become something of a legend, eluding capture for a long time. Now it seemed Wyatt's luck had run out.

Wyatt strode past Brand's cell, staring straight ahead, his mouth set in a taut line. He was grey with dust, his face battered and bloody. The scar on his face gleamed stark white against his darker flesh. He looked as mean and hard as his reputation suggested.

Willard Beal's deputy, Rick Lander, was behind Wyatt. He marched the outlaw to the end cell and locked him inside.

"Appears you've caught yourself a load of trouble there, boy," Brand said as Rick made his way back to the office.

Rick paused at Brand's cell. His young face was bitter. He made no attempt to conceal his contempt for Jason Brand. In Rick's eyes Brand was a disgrace to the profession. He knew about Brand's past career. He also figured Brand was nothing more than a hired gun now. In Rick's eyes that made Brand no better than Ben Wyatt.

"I can handle him," Rick stated cooly.

"I hope you're right, boy. Just

remember Wyatt runs with a hard bunch. His boys ain't about to ride on and forget you got Wyatt locked up. You and Beal are going to have to stay sharp."

Rick's face hardened. He stepped close to the cell.

"Damn you, Brand. Will Beal is dead. Gunned down by Wyatt's bunch. And a son of a bitch like you figures he can tell me how to run this office."

"Sorry about Will," Brand said. "But you're alive, boy, and you've got Ben Wyatt in your jail. I don't give a damn how you feel about me. You just think on. Wyatt's no drunken cowhand having himself a ball on a Saturday night. This one's a killer, boy. The kind you only hope to hear about once in a lifetime. His bunch is just as bad. His brother, Al, is a mad dog. They put their mind to it they'll burn this town to the ground to get Wyatt out."

Rick listened in silence. He would never admit it, but deep down he knew that Brand was right. Ben Wyatt's reputation had gone before him. There were few who didn't know what Wyatt was capable of. Rick knew and the knowledge scared the hell out of him.

Brand watched the young Deputy leave and close the door to the office. He had said his piece and that was an end to it. Rick would have to stand or fall by his own actions. He was young and up to now he'd only experienced the easy side of keeping the law. Now he would find there was more to it than wearing a shiny badge and carrying a big gun on his hip. If an experienced lawman like Will Beal had fallen to Wyatt's bunch how was a comparative novice like Rick going to fare?

Brand returned to his cot, his back to the wall. It was none of his business. Adobe had to handle its own problems. He thought briefly of Will Beal. Sorry that the man was dead, but knowing that Beal himself would have accepted the risks of the job. The possibility of being killed on duty came with the territory, and any man who pinned on a badge was a fool if he deluded himself otherwise.

Some while later he became aware of raised voices coming from the office beyond the cell area. He couldn't make out what was being said, but there was some hard talking being done. The arguments raged for long minutes and then an abrupt silence fell. Moments later the door opened and Rick appeared. He walked stiff legged to Brand's cell and unlocked it. As the door swung open Brand suddenly realised what was happening.

"In the office," Rick said coldy.

Brand snatched up his hat and made his way through to the office.

Judge Rice was there, sitting behind Will Beal's desk. There were others too. Solemn, dark-suited men. Brand recognised them as the town's men of power. Adobe's ruling body. Men who had the money and influence.

Judge Rice a slender, whitehaired man in his late fifties motioned for

Brand to sit down.

"Do I need to spell it out for you?" Rice asked.

Brand settled back in his seat. "Wyatt in the cells. His boys close by. Adobe's heading for trouble."

"You hear about Will Beal?"

Brand nodded. "I heard."

"We've just learned that George Cagle, the other deputy is dead too. He stopped a bullet inthe gunfight outside the bank."

Brand glanced in Rick's direction. The young deputy was staring blindly out the window. *Poor bastard*, he thought. The boy had been put right on the line.

"I'm inclined to agree about Wyatt's bunch being close by," Rice said. "The fact we have him locked up isn't going to deter them for long."

Brand didn't reply. He was taking a look at the faces around him. There was contempt in some eyes, which didn't bother Brand in the slightest. Because he knew what was on the other side of the coin. Adobe needed him far more than he needed the town. They needed his experience. His skill with a gun, and his affinity with violence. It was a sad thing to have to admit to, but they were Brand's stock in trade, and he was if nothing else, a practical man. He realised he was in an enviable position. If the notion took him he could bleed the town dry and make them crawl before he gave them what they wanted.

Judge Rice was watching Brand. Returning the Judge's shrewd gaze Brand was certain he saw a faint glimmer of a smile play around the edges of the man's mouth. Rice knew exactly what Brand was thinking, and he was waiting to see how Brand played the game.

"I'll say this once," the Judge stated. "Beal is dead. The only law we have in town is Rick Lander. He's been a deputy for four months. There isn't a man in this room who doubts Rick's loyalty, or his courage. However it would be unfair of us to expect him to face the Wyatt bunch on his own. I for one won't ask him to do that."

Judge Rice opened a drawer and took out a rolled gunbelt. He placed it on the desk in front of Brand. Next to it he placed a silver star.

"The gun is your own, Brand. The badge is Will Beal's. You both walked the same line."

Brand fingered the badge. "One dead and one who got himself kicked out of a job. That tell you something about the job, Judge?"

"Spare me the self pity," Rice snapped. "I don't accept you're as cynical as you make out. Added to that is the fact I've been a gambler all my life. A man has to be to exist in this damn country. I'm willing to bet on you."

"I like to know what I'm playing for," Brand said. "Could be a safer option for me to sit out my fourteen days."

Rice shook his head. "Not you,

Brand. You might not give a damn about Adobe — but you won't walk away from the situation."

Rick Lander turned away from the window. "Talk to him in his language, Judge. Tell him how much the job's worth."

"Easy, boy," Brand soothed. "We've all got a price."

"Eight thousand dollars," Rice said, placing a long buff envelope on the desk. "The town will pay your expenses, and there's a room in back you can use."

"And I get a free hand to run things my way?"

"Guaranteed."

"*Now hold on, Caleb!*"

Brand glanced at the speaker. He was a big man, running to fat, his pink jowls sagging over the collar of his white shirt.

"Something sticking in your craw?" Brand asked.

"All this talk about giving you a free hand. I take that to mean you want to

33

run this office any way you see fit?"

"It's the only way," Brand said. "One man wears the badge and he's in charge. He makes the rules and plays the game."

"The hell you say, Brand," the fat man protested, jabbing a finger at the ex-US Marshal. "You expect us to hand over our town to a disgraced lawman and a drunk, and let him do just what he wants, Caleb?"

"It's your town that's in trouble, mister. If Wyatt's bunch ride and burn it down I'm not going to lose a damn thing." Brand took the badge and offered it to the fat man. "You want to stop them? Here, take this and save Adobe eight thousand dollars."

The man drew back, his face quivering with righteous anger.

"I'm no gunman. I'm a businessman. When I need a job doing I go out and hire someone. That's what the eight thousand is for, Brand. It buys you."

Brand came up off his seat, his face darkening with rage. For a split-second it looked as if he was going to hit the fat man. But he held himself back, and when he spoke his voice was flat and cold.

"No way, friend. You figure your money can buy you anything you want? Well not this body. All that money does is hire me and my gun for a limited period. When you buy something you own it. Well you don't own me, mister, and I ain't about to jump when you snap your fingers. You want your town off the hook? Fine. Just stay out of my way and let me do the job."

Brand picked up his gunbelt and strapped it on. He picked up the envelope, opened it, and ran a finger across the wad of banknotes.

"Gentlemen, consider me hired. Now do me a favour and get the hell out of here. Give me a chance to see what I can do about saving your town."

The group filed out, avoiding his gaze. Brand closed the door behind them. He turned back into the office and saw that Judge Rice was still seated behind the desk.

"How do you put up with them?" Brand asked.

Rice shrugged. "They own most of the town is why. We don't all bite the hand that feeds us," he added wryly.

Brand grunted. "Wonder who's worst? That bunch or Wyatt's boys."

"Most folk in Adobe are honest and hardworking. They're the ones who need the help."

"Yeah," Brand mumbled. He crossed over to the stove and helped himself to a mugful of coffee from the blackened pot standing on the stove.

"You setting a trial date, Judge?" he asked.

"Day after tomorrow. I need that time to organise."

"Any chance of quashing my sentence at the same time?"

Rice chuckled. "I forgot to mention that was part of the deal. You're already a free man."

"You think so?" Brand asked in all

seriousness. He might have been out of his cell — but he was still a prisoner of his own destiny, trapped within the circle of the gun and his ability to use it to such deadly effect.

"Rick."

The deputy glanced at Brand, indecision on his face.

"You going to stick? Or are you figuring on quitting?"

"Quit? Hell, no," Rick said. He faced Brand squarely. "I want to be there when Wyatt's bunch ride you into the ground."

Brand, pinning on Will Beal's badge, raised his eyes to Rick's face. "You stay that way, boy. Good and mad. Maybe it'll give us both the chance to ride this thing through."

3

"ONE of us in the office all the time," Brand said. "The door stays locked and if we're not sure who's trying to get in, it doesn't get opened."

Rick Lander listened in silence to Brand's instructions. He hadn't said very much since Judge Rice had left. Brand was aware that the deputy was sizing him up. Rick needed time, so Brand just let it run its own course.

"We can have meals sent in. You know the town so I'll let you fix it. In fact do it now. Then take a stroll round town. Give me a chance to look this place over."

Rick picked up his hat and made for the door.

"Take this," Brand said, handing Rick the rifle he had just loaded. "From now on we go prepared for trouble."

"You're the boss," Rick said sharply.

"Right," Brand replied. "Rick, you got any idea how many of Wyatt's boys got clear?"

"Seven rode in. We shot two out on the street. Wyatt's in back. So that leaves four."

"Enough," Brand said softly.

He locked the door behind Rick. Watched the deputy through the barred window as he crossed the street and went into a restaurant. At least the boy took orders. That could make a difference when trouble did show.

Brand made his way through to the cells. At the top end of the passage was a heavy, iron-banded door that led into the alley at the side of the jail. There were heavy bolts securing it at the top and bottom. To one side were the jail's living quarters. Here Brand found two small rooms. They were cheerless places, containing little in the way of furnishings. Each had a small window, high up and heavily barred. One of the rooms was Rick's. The other would have been Will Beal's. Brand stood in the doorway. There was a bed and a chair. A small clothes chest. A few personal items were scattered about the spare room. It typified a lawman's lot. He sacrificed a great deal for the Spartan existence of his profession. The job promised a life of danger, with little reward, and expected the lawman to live like a monk. Brand stared around the bleak room, asking himself the question he'd voiced a hundred times before. *Why?* Why did a man choose to spend his life like this? Giving up home and families for the most part. Isolating himself from those around him, because the strictures of the job demanded he not allow himself to become beholden to anyone. The work made a man a loner. A solitary, often friendless figure. For what? Poor pay and unsociable hours. And in many cases a short life with a violent end. Will Beal had been an example of that extreme. Yet most lawmen shrugged off the bleaker aspects of their profession and carried on without complaint. Jason Brand was no better himself. He might have lost his status as a US Marshal, but he found he still functioned within the same code of ethics. He would have felt stifled in any other occupation. Not that there was much else he could do. His job was his life. It was the only thing he knew.

Brand walked along the passage until he was standing outside Wyatt's cell. The outlaw was sitting on his cot. He stared at Brand for a moment until he recognised who he was looking at. Then he came up off the cot, lunging for the bars of the cell door.

"What the hell is this?" he yelled. "You were in a cell when they brought me in. How'd you get that badge?"

"I've got it and that's all you need to know, Wyatt. One other thing. There's no way you're getting out of that cell except for when you go to trial and probably when they hang you. Forget about that crew of yours coming to break you out. It won't happen. I'm no kid deputy, and I'm not Will Beal."

"Well, the hell with you, mister," Wyatt said. "I'll be out of here sooner than you think. And I'll see you dead 'fore I burn this damn town to the ground."

Brand left the outlaw still cursing and returned to the office. He poured himself another coffee and sat at the desk. Now he was inactive he became aware of the headache still pulsing inside his skull. What he needed was a good meal inside him. Then a bath and a change of clothing. He ran his hand over his face — and a shave.

Someone knocked on the outer door. Brand crossed to it.

"Yeah?"

"I'm from the restaurant across the street," a female voice said. "Rick said I should bring you some food, Marshal Brand."

Brand unlocked the door and eased it open. His Colt was in his hand by this time. "Bring it inside."

42

A figure carrying a cloth-covered tray stepped inside. Brand closed the door and locked it.

"Put it on the desk," he said.

He watched the woman place the tray on the desk. She looked to be in her late twenties. A redhead, wearing a snug fitting blue-check dress. When she turned to face him he saw she was attractive rather than beautiful. Her eyes were wide and deep green, and they looked him over with unexpected boldness. She had a firm, full mouth and high cheekbones. The body under the dress was strong and shapely.

"Tell me, Marshal Brand, do you do everything with a gun in your hand?" she asked, a faintly mocking tone to her question.

Brand put the gun away. "No," he said. "Not everything. What do they call you?"

"Why? Are you going to arrest me?"

He grinned at her. Taking the cloth off the tray he saw a a large plate holding a thick steak, fried potatoes

43

and a couple of eggs. On a smaller plate were slices of fresh bread.

"You cook this?"

She nodded. Then her smooth face was marred by a frown. "Is there going to be trouble?"

"Could be." Brand sat down and began to eat, realising just how hungry he was.

"The way people are talking about you it sounds like you'll be able to handle it."

"That what they're saying?"

"Yes." She was starting to become uneasy now, not certain how she stood in the eyes of this man of violence.

"Maybe you shouldn't believe everything you hear."

"I make up my own mind," she said defensively. "I'll pick up the tray later. If I stay too long people will start talking. Damn! I didn't mean to say that."

"Does it bother you what people say?"

She held his gaze, flushing slightly.

"I . . . *no* . . . it doesn't bother me."

Brand walked her to the door. He unlocked it, his Colt back in his hand.

"In certain circumstances that thing could be downright off-putting," she suggested.

Brand pulled open the door and she stepped outside, pausing to brush stray hair back from her face.

"By the way my name is Abigail. Most folk call me Abby."

Brand watched her cross the street and vanish inside the restaurant. He closed the jail door, locking it behind him. Returning to the meal Abby had brought he concentrated on eating. Taking a second cup of coffee he stood up and crossed to the window, staring out across the street.

Adobe appeared to be going about its everyday business. There was little to show what the town was actually going through. Brand did notice, however, that the jail seemed to be attracting a fair share of stares.

He glanced at the clock on the

office wall. It was coming up to noon. Time was starting to drag now. Waiting was as much an enemy as any man with a gun in his hand. They were all waiting for something to happen. Brand thought about Wyatt's bunch. They'd be out there somewhere close by. Biding their time. Watching and waiting. Looking out for any pursuit. For any sign they were being searched for. Brand had no intention of going along that road. Wyatt's bunch was too wily to let itself get trapped by any trigger-happy posse of over-excited townspeople. As far as Brand was concerned he would sit it out and wait for them to make their move. There was no way he'd know what they intended until the time came. Then he would handle it.

Rick appeared on the street, returning to the jail. By the time the young deputy reached the door Brand had it unlocked. He motioned Rick inside, then secured the door again.

"Any problems?"

"Only a feeling."

"Hang on to that, boy. Feelings are what make a good lawman. Being able to trust your instincts. You figure there's something on the wind?"

"Could be. Town's all wound up tight."

Brand put his hat on. Picked up a loaded rifle.

"I might be a while. Need to get cleaned up some. Then I'll take a walk round town. Show my face. You keep this door locked. Before you open it to anyone — think hard. If something doesn't smell right keep the door between you and it. Don't trust anybody. Remember one chance is all you get."

Leaving the jail Brand made his way uptown. The day was hot and still. Dust puffed up from under his boots as he crossed the street. He went into a store. When he came out some minutes later he had a wrapped bundle under his arm. His next stop was at the barbershop and the bath house out back. He had a long soak, then got the barber to shave him. Afterwards he dressed in the new shirt and pants he'd bought. There was a dark vest to go with the outfit and Brand pinned his badge to it.

As he made a steady tour of the town he was aware of the close scrutiny he was receiving. There were those who made their feelings plain the way they stared through him. Brand ignored them. He found a large percentage of Adobe's population were there to wish him well. Over it all there was a definite air of tension. Rick had been right. There was something in the wind.

He found himself drawn to the saloons. If there was trouble brewing it would be fermenting in one of the saloons. Drink helped a man gather his courage, even though it might well be false, and would vanish when he sobered up. But in the crowded and heady atmosphere of a noisy saloon a man could become a conspirator with ease.

He stopped outside *The Adobe Palace*. It was the town's largest and most popular establishment. Right now it was very noisy. Brand went up on the boardwalk and in through the swing doors, pausing inside to allow his eyes to adjust to the subdued light. He scanned the place, searching the blur of faces and voices. He knew he'd come to the right place. The feeling was already nibbling away at his gut. The feeling was almost as thick as the pale curls of smoke drifting to lodge in amongst the dusty beams in the roof. Brand moved into the saloon, and as his presence was noticed a silence fell over the crowd.

"Any problems, Marshal?"

The speaker, a stocky, darkhaired man dressed in a pearl grey suit, with a white shirt and maroon cravat, exuded confidence — and money.

"Just checking." Brand faced the man. "You are?"

"Phil Hoyt. This is my place." In a lower tone Hoyt said: "I think you ought to know, Marshal. There's been some talk about a lynching party. Some of the local ranch hands. They can be a pretty rough bunch once the drink gets to the spot."

"They still around?"

Hoyt nodded. "The group at the far end of the bar. The big man in the yellow shirt — Bart Rimbaund — he's the leader. Take my word, Marshal, he's a mean one."

Brand nodded. "Thanks, Hoyt," he said and pushed his way through the crowd as he approached the far end of the long bar. He took his time sizing up the bunch Hoyt had identified. They *were* a hard looking bunch. Clad in their range gear, with heavy guns on their hips, they gave the impression of being indestructible. Brand didn't let himself be fooled. These men would be hard. They had to be for the job they did.

"Hey, boys, take off your hats, 'cause

the new lawman is come to visit!"

It was Rimbaund himself who spoke. He was big. Broad across the shoulders, with a massive chest and lean hips. Brand didn't miss his hands. They were large and big-knuckled, the flesh scarred and calloused. Rimbaund's dark, feral eyes studied Brand closely.

"I hear you boys are planning to do me out of my job," Brand said conversationally.

Rimbaund grinned. His large teeth stood out against his tanned face. "You could say that, Marshal. Just me and the boys figuring to save the town the price of a trial. Wyatt's guilty so what's the use of wasting the court's time?"

Brand sighed. He knew Rimbaund of old. Big, tough, and mean. There was one in every town. They hated authority. They disliked the law and would do anything liable to upset it. The Bart Rimbaunds of the world operated on a simple premise. Be with me and it'll be fine. Be against me you got a war on your hands.

"I'll say this once, Rimbaund. Stay away from the jail. There won't be any lynching while I'm wearing this badge."

Rimbaund laughed, and the sound was heavy in the silent saloon. As he laughed Rimbaund cuffed his hat to the back of his head.

"Looks like we have to forget the hanging, boys. The new Marshal says no."

There was a chorus of harsh laughter from Rimbaund's companions.

"*Stay away?*" Rimbaund said, the humour fading as quickly as it had come. "Mister, when I decide to come for Wyatt you stay out of my way. You hear?" He thrust his broad face close to Brand's. "You hear me, pissant?"

Brand heard him. And decided he didn't like Rimbaund's attitude. So he hit him. Driving the stock of his rifle into the big man's stomach, Brand put all his weight behind the blow. Rimbaund gasped, his face darkening. Brand shouldered him away from the bar, laying the barrel of the rifle across Rimbaund's jaw. The cowman staggered, blood streaking the line of his thick jaw. As Brand eased away from him he caught a glimpse of one of Rimbaund's group lunging at him. He half-turned, swinging the rifle round in a swift arc that whacked the man across the side of the head, spinning him back against the bar where he stood clutching both hands to his bleeding skull. Brand pushed his back to the bar as the saloon erupted with noise. Chairs were hastily shoved away from tables, boots clattering on the plank floor as the area near the bar was cleared.

"First to move gets a bullet," Brand yelled. He had the rifle primed and ready, the muzzle held unwavering on Rimbaund and his bunch.

Rimbaund himself had slumped to his knees, his head down against his chest. Blood dripped to the floor from his face.

"Any more trouble I'll fill some empty cells," Brand said. "This town's had enough grief for one day. Let it lie. Now finish your drinks and get the hell out of here."

He turned away from them, moving out across the saloon, passing the rifle to his left hand. The silence held, men moving aside as Brand approached.

He was close to the swing doors when his ear picked up the faint click of a gun hammer going back.

Brand dropped into a crouch, turning, his right hand snaking the big Colt from its holster. His thumb dogged the hammer back. As he came around a gun roared, the bullet ripping pale splinters of wood from the doorframe just above his head. Brand's gun arm levelled, the Colt's muzzle seeking and finding its target. He had the shooter pinpointed now. It was the man he'd hit across the side of the head with his rifle. The man was already easing back the hammer of his revolver for a second shot. Brand didn't hesitate. The time for discussion had been lost. He touched the Colt's trigger, driving a single bullet into the other's chest. The heavy chunk of lead ripped through the man's body and tore a fist-sized hole on its way out. The dying man twisted to one side, hitting a table as he went down, scattering bottles and glasses across the floor.

Rimbaund, lurching to his feet, made a grab for his own gun. "*You son of a bitch!*" he screamed.

"Go ahead," Brand said. "Give me the excuse I need, Rimbaund."

Rimbaund stared at Brand's levelled Colt, then at the face above the weapon, and decided he was holding a losing hand. He let his hand ease away from the gun on his hip. He sleeved blood away from his jawline.

"I can wait, Brand."

"So can I," Brand said and left the saloon.

He crossed the street, elbowing his way through the gathering crowd. He was angry with himself. At the way things had turned out. *Damn Rimbaund!* The man had been determined to push his way into trouble. Now a man was dead.

Brand spotted Judge Rice near the courthouse and crossed to speak to him.

"Problems?" Rice asked.

"I had to kill a man," Brand said. "Don't ask if it solved anything. It just meant I stayed alive and he didn't. But he pushed and I had to push back."

"What started it?"

"Fellow by the name of Rimbaund figured to save the town the cost of a trial by lynching Wyatt."

"Bart Rimbaund? If you've crossed swords with that man, Brand, don't close your eyes for a second. Rimbaund is mean through and through. He was born vicious. He's a bad man to have against you."

"I'll bear that in mind."

Rice sighed. "The sooner we get this trial over with the better I'll like it. The longer it drags on the more chance there is of Bart Rimbaund and his cronies causing trouble."

After he'd finished talking with the Judge Brand returned to the jail. He knocked on the door and identified himself to Rick's challenge. The deputy opened the door and let him in. Brand tossed his hat on the desk and laid down the rifle. He slumped in the chair behind the desk and watched as Rick bolted the door.

"I heard the shooting," Rick said. "You involved."

"You might say. Get me some coffee, Rick."

While the deputy poured the coffee Brand told him what had happened. Rick placed the steaming mug on the desk.

"Always happens when Rimbaund and his crew are in town. He goes out of his way to find trouble. Like he has to prove how tough he is all the time." Rick hesitated, then added: "You should have shot Rimbaund. Long as he's around the others follow."

Brand glanced at the office clock.

"You eaten yet?"

Rick shook his head "Not since breakfast."

"Go now. And have something sent over for Wyatt."

Rick nodded. He took his rifle and left the office.

Brand bolted the door. He took a look at Wyatt. The outlaw was stretched out on his bunk, seemingly asleep. Brand returned to the office, staring out of the window. The day would be gone soon, he thought. He wondered if it would be a cloudless night with a good moon. If not the darkness would offer cover for anyone out for mischief. Like Wyatt's bunch. Or Bart Rimbaund and his rope-hungry crew.

The problems were starting to pile up. On top of everything else there would be an inquest into the death of the man Brand had shot. The Judge had pointed this out to Brand. It would only be a formality, he'd explained. As far as Brand was concerned it was a pain in the ass. He drained his coffee and stared into the empty mug. Life would be a lot simpler if problems were as easily emptied away.

4

THE foothills of the Gilas were hard and rocky. Vegetation was scarce. In the main it was cactus, though there was a mix of mesquite and cholla. Here and there stiff clumps of bleached grass survived despite the rigors of the climate. The landscape was one of ridges and gullies. Rock and sand. Towering sandstone bluffs and deep, shadowed canyons. The sun hung over this silent land, bathing it in unrelenting heat that caused shimmering waves. Sometimes a dry, dusty wind would whisper its hot way across the land, stirring the grasses and the paloverde.

Jake Sutter had led them into a narrow canyon that wormed its way deep into the foothills. Here they were able to rest. The horses were unsaddled and tethered close to a shallow stream that meandered across the canyon floor. One of the group climbed to a high vantage point and watched for sign of any pursuit while the others made camp.

With Ben Wyatt back in Adobe and two others shot dead during the escape, there were only four of them left. There was Sutter himself. Al Wyatt. A lean, pale-haired individual named Billy Reece; Reece was a gunslinger who had hung around the fringes of the Clanton gang during the bloody days in Tombstone before the legendary shootout with the Earps and Doc Holliday at the OK Corral back in '81; with foresight unusual for his breed Reece had seen the writing on the wall, and he had departed Tombstone two days before the gunfight. Following a period of going it alone Reece had joined up with Ben Wyatt. He favoured Wyatt's way of running things and had settled well within the group. The fourth member of the surviving group, now on watch, was a half-breed Apache named Silvano; he was a solitary, self-sufficient figure, not given much to talking. He was, though, a superb tracker and deadly with gun or knife.

Putting Silvano up in the high rocks was purely a precautionary measure on Jake Sutter's part. He didn't really expect any kind of pursuit from Adobe. The town had lost its law and had been left with Ben Wyatt on its hands. That was enough for any town to handle. Sutter couldn't imagine any individual wanting to head up some rag-tag collection of glory seekers taking up the chase — especially when it came down to tackling the Wyatt bunch in the heart of the Gila Mountains.

Al Wyatt had wanted to turn right around and charge back to Adobe to free Ben the moment he realised what had happened. It had taken Sutter some time to calm him down and explain that it made better sense to wait for the right time. Adobe needed to calm down. For the townspeople to relax. Let their guard down a little. Anyone going in too soon was liable to be shot on sight by some nervous storekeeper carrying a gun.

So they sat out the rest of the day in the canyon. It was only after a couple of hours that Sutter remembered the saddlebags he had carried with him from Adobe. They all gathered round as he tipped the contents onto a blanket and made a count.

It came to eleven thousand dollars.

"*Christ!*" Al raged. "Two of our boys dead. Ben in a stinking cell. And all we end up with is eleven thousand dollars!" He kicked out at the stack of banknotes, scattering the money across the ground.

"Cut that out, Al," Sutter yelled. He was getting heartily tired of Al and his childlike tantrums. Ben's brother or no, Al was heading for trouble.

"And you quit telling me what to do!" Al rounded on Sutter, his face taut, mouth trembling with emotion.

"You ain't in charge. Ben is *my* brother."

"Well if I ain't in charge, sonny, it sure as hell don't put you in the damn ring," Sutter said calmly. "So sit down and keep your mouth shut. We've got a long ride tonight if we're going to bust Ben out of that jail."

"The hell I'm going to sit down, Sutter. I'm tired of listening to you bossin' everyone around, just 'cause you put out the tale you're good with that fancy gun you carry."

Billy Reece glanced up from the mug of coffee he was drinking, his mouth half open. He couldn't be certain he'd heard right. Had Al actually questioned Jake Sutter's ability with a gun? He must have, Reece realised, when he caught the expression on Sutter's face. The Texan had drawn himself upright, his lean body ramrod stiff. His right hand was drifting close to the black butt of his holstered Remington. *My God*, Reece thought, *he's going to shoot Al's balls off!* Reece glanced at

64

Al, and saw with surprise that Al was actually grinning. The kid thought it was all so damned simple. He probably even thought he could outdraw Jake Sutter. Reece found he was wishing it would happen so that Sutter could kill the whining little pissant. It was only because of Ben that Sutter was holding back.

"I always knew you were yellow, Sutter," Al shrilled, his voice high and excited like an overheated schoolgirl. "You're all horseshit!"

The words were barely out of Al's mouth when Jake Sutter moved with a suddenness that startled even Billy Reece. Sutter's long stride took him to where Al stood, and the bewildered expression that crossed Al's face was lost in a smear of blood when Sutter drove his big fist into it. The hard blow slammed Al back against the canyon wall. He stood there, seemingly unable to move, his eyes wide and showing naked fear. A faint whimper burst from his crushed and bloody lips as

Sutter stepped in close. The tall Texan moved deliberately, slamming his left fist into Al's stomach. The crippling blow ripped a loud squeal from Al. He arched away from the canyon side, clutching himself. Sutter let him walk forward, then clubbed a solid blow to the side of Al's head. The impact drove Al to his knees. Sutter drove the toe of his boot into Al's side, putting deadly force into the kick, flipping Al over on his back. Then he bent over Al and grabbed him by the shirtfront, hauling him to his feet. Then he began to hit Al, in the face and body, until there was little point in carrying on. When Sutter finally let go Al dropped to the ground and lay there.

"Boy, you've been asking for that a long time. Trouble with Ben he's too damn soft with you. And don't worry none about telling him who done it. I'll tell him myself."

Al lay where he was for a long time. His whole body hurt. It felt as if it was on fire, and he was trembling violently, almost as if he was freezing. He knew it was from fear. That angered him more than anything. *Damn you Jake Sutter!* Al's need for revenge washed over the pain and he contented himself with planning a terrible way of repaying Sutter. Maybe Ben himself would help. Then he reconsidered, deciding that Ben would refuse to harm Jake Sutter. Ben trusted Sutter and depended on him too much. *Well damn 'em all!* Al figured he would kill Sutter himself. In his own time and in his own way. Then it would be his turn to laugh. An unreasoning rage grew inside Al. It was directed towards Ben. His brother should have been here. Then his beating at Sutter's hands wouldn't have happened. He realised that for the first time in his life Ben wasn't around to advise and protect him. It was a new experience for Al Wyatt, and he wasn't sure he liked it. He had to get Ben out of jail. The sooner the better. Before the town of Adobe hung him.

Al rolled his eyes skywards, wishing the day would end and night would cover the land. It had to come soon — and when it did he could ride back to Adobe and free Ben.

5

BRAND saw to it that every rifle in the wall rack was fully loaded. He dealt similarly with his own weapons. While he was attending to the guns, Rick Lander lit the lamps in the office. When all that had been done they made a final tour of the jail, checking every window and door.

"You're looking a touch nervous, Marshal," Ben Wyatt said as Brand passed his cell.

Brand turned to face him. "Nervous?" He shook his head. "Isn't me they're going to hang, Wyatt."

"Tough man, huh? Well you'll need to be when my boys come for me."

Brand returned to the office, closing the door to the cell block. Rick was stoking the stove. Outside the light was fading fast, shadows lengthening. Checking the sky Brand saw that clouds were still hanging low in the sky.

"I'll take my tour now," Brand said, picking up his rifle.

Rick followed him to the door, unbolting it.

"Bart Rimbaund is still in town."

Brand checked the rifle. "Figured he would be. Rimbaund has a one-track mind. Only thing liable to get him off it is a bullet."

Outside Brand waited until he heard Rick lock the door. It was still warm, the day's heat lingering. From beyond town a breeze wafted the scent of sage along the street. Adobe gave the appearance of settling down. Most of the businesses had closed early. Only a few still showed lights. At the far end of the street there was plenty of light showing from the saloons.

Lodging the rifle in the crook of his arm Brand moved away from the jail. He found himself glancing across the street in the direction of the restaurant where Abby worked. He felt a need to see her again, and from the way she had reacted earlier he felt his attentions would be welcomed. Not that he had much time for socialising right now. Peace and quiet were in short supply in Adobe at the present time.

He was well on his way along the street when the realisation came that here he was wearing a badge again. Carrying out the duties of a lawman as if he'd never been away. He had slipped back into the role with little conscious effort. Without conceit Brand realised he would have been surprised if the return had caused him any problems. The old saying about once a lawman, always a lawman, certainly held true as far as he was concerned. The location was different perhaps. Another town in another place, but that meant little. Cause and effect were exactly the same. He had been a lawman for too long. It was in his blood, as it had always been, and there was nothing that was going to change it. Judge Rice had known it, and that was why he had made Brand the offer. The Judge had been canny enough to know Brand wouldn't refuse. Given longer to think about it Brand might have declined — but the situation in Adobe had become too immediate, requiring a strong hand to keep it in check. Truth was Brand and the badge were one. There was no way out of that. He had the scars from all his long years upholding the law. There were the physical scars and there were the invisible ones, deeply etched on his mind. They existed in order to remind him that he knew his profession and the dangers any given situation might present.

He reached the limit of his patrol, turned and made his way along the far side of the street, checking doors and alleys. As he drew level with the restaurant the door opened and Abby herself stepped outside. As she closed the door behind her Brand caught a glimpse of the interior. Most of the tables were occupied and Brand picked up the rich aroma of food and coffee. Then Abby closed the door, smiling as she recognised him.

"Why, Marshal, have you come to walk me home?"

"Depends how far," he told her.

"Just a little way along the street."

"Then it'll be my pleasure."

She looked him over as they fell in step.

"All shaved. New clothes. You look very impressive." Her eyes sparkled. "I see you still have your gun with you. I hope it isn't my presence that causes all this insecurity."

He chuckled softly. "Last thing I feel when you're around is insecure."

"Oh? And just what emotion do I stir, Jason Brand?"

She paused and turned to face him, putting out a slim hand to touch his arm. For a long, silent moment she stared into his face.

"*Well?*"

"Abby . . . I . . . "

"Why don't you just kiss me," she suggested.

"Because, damnit, it might not stop

there," he said gruffly.

"I'm prepared to take the chance."

She leaned in towards him, breasts nudging him gently. Brand slipped an arm around her slim waist, drawing her close, feeling the curve of her thighs against his. She pressed her soft mouth to his, willingly, lips parting moistly. She flicked the tip of her tongue against his teeth in a playful gesture. Brand kissed her hard, aware he was bruising her lips, but enjoying her unrestrained response.

"Jason, maybe we should . . . " Abby began as she eventually drew away, flushed and slightly breathless.

And then she caught a glimpse of his face in the half-light. Saw the sudden change that had come over him. His features had hardened, the flesh drawn tautly over his cheekbones. There was a brittle chill in his eyes. Without warning he grabbed her arm, roughly, and pushed her to the boardwalk.

"And stay down!" he said harshly, spinning away from her, his rifle leaping into his hands. It roared, spitting a gout of flame and powdersmoke into the night. Somewhere in the gloom a man screamed in pain. There was the sound of a body hitting the ground. Following on this came a solid blast of gunfire from the opposite side of the street. By this time Brand was down on the boardwalk himself, flat on his belly. He was moving the rifle's muzzle back and forth, searching for more targets. Bullets whacked the store front over his head. The display window shattered, showering him and Abby with glass. Brand returned fire, aiming for the distant muzzle blasts. He didn't wait to see if he had scored any hits. Rising to his feet he reached out and snatched for Abby's hand. He half-dragged her along the boardwalk, barely giving her time to gain her feet. Bullets smacked into the woodwork around them, filling the air with flying splinters. Reaching the closest alley he shoved Abby off the boardwalk into the covering darkness. As he followed her into the alley more bullets chewed at the corner of the building.

"Who is it?" Abby demanded angrily. "Why are they shooting . . . hey, quit pushing, Jason . . ."

He ignored her. There was no time for talk now. He could hear the sound of pounding boots as the gunmen came across the street in the direction of the alley. Brand grabbed Abby's arm again, pushing her ahead of him along the alley. When she hesitated he gave her an almighty shove that sent her staggering forward. This time she took his advice and ran, picking up her skirts. Close on her heels Brand followed, glancing back over his shoulder to check how close their pursuers were. He spotted dark shapes darting into the alley. Skidding to a halt he turned, shouldering the rifle and triggering a rapid volley of shots at the moving shadows. He heard one man yell in pain, saw the figures pull back. Trailing Abby he pulled spare cartridges from his pants pocket and thumbed them into the rifle's slot.

He heard someone shout from the far side of the street, then heard shots, followed by a series of heavy crashing sounds.

The jail!

They were trying for the jail. And Rick Lander was on his own.

"This way, Abby," he said as they reached the far end of the alley.

He had to get back to the jail fast. He didn't want to leave Abby on her own, but he had little choice. He cursed the luck that had brought them together in the wrong place at the wrong time.

They skirted the rear of a building, then the next. Brand peered down the alley running between the pair of buildings. It would bring him on to the street directly opposite the jail. Without hesitation Brand caught hold of Abby's hand and pulled her in his wake as he ran for the mouth of the alley. They had just reached the street end when a shot rang out from their rear. Brand heard Abby gasp, then felt the pull of her hand as she stumbled. He held her upright, turning to face the way they'd come, and saw the dark outline of a running man coming along the alley. As the man passed through a pool of light cast by a window Brand saw he was one of the men who had been with Rimbaund in the saloon. He also saw the raised gun in the man's hand. Bracing the rifle against his hip Brand fired a single shot that caught the man in mid-stride. His head jerked back, blood flying in a dark spray.

"Damn, it hurts," Abby muttered fiercely. She sagged against him, suddenly giving in to the weakness flooding her body. Brand drew her close as he pressed against the wall at the extreme end of the alley.

The door to the jail stood wide open. It was a rectangle of light in the darkness, and he could see moving figures in the office. *Damn them!* They just never knew when to leave things alone.

He eased Abby to the ground, against

the wall of the building.

"Stay right there," he said. "Don't move. I'll be back."

He held the rifle at the ready, then broke away from the mouth of the ally and cut across the street. His only thought was to get inside the jail. He heard shouts. Shots rang out. Bullets kicked up gouts of dust from the street around him. Brand ran on, oblivious to the danger. He let out a shocked gasp as one bullet burned across his left arm. Then he was on the boardwalk, his momentum taking him across the porch and in through the wide open door of the jail.

The office was in a mess. The desk on its side. Chairs thrown across the floor. As his gaze took in the scene Brand saw Rick Lander hunched in a corner. There was blood over his face and down his shirt. Anger rose in Brand, adding a wild recklessness to his actions.

He had spotted two of Rimbaund's men at the door leading through to the cells. As he had burst into the office they had turned, surprise in their eyes when they recognised him. Brand gave them little chance to react further. He tipped up the muzzle of the rifle and shot the closest through the body. The man bounced off the wall, leaving a smear of blood on the plaster as he went down. As his partner fell the second man began to turn, clawing for the gun on his hip. Brand, still moving forward, smashed the barrel of the Winchester down across the man's wrist. Bone snapped and the man yelled in agony, the sound cutting off abruptly as Brand reversed the rifle and clubbed him across the side of the head with the hard stock, driving him to the floor. Stepping over the downed men Brand lunged into the passage beyond. There were three men before him. Rimbaund himself was struggling to find the right key for Wyatt's cell, while the other two stood watch. As Brand appeared he met this pair head on. He saw lamplight gleam on a raised gun barrel and swung his body aside. He felt the wall at his back, using it as a lever to catapult himself into the man with the raised weapon. Closing in fast Brand drove the rifle into the man's exposed stomach, then jammed his knee into his groin. The man howled in agony, clutching his hurt body. Turning on his heel Brand spotted the second man jumping towards him. He caught a hard blow on the side of his head, another stunning punch that tore a gash over his right cheek. Brand swayed back from the impact, though he barely felt the pain. As the man came in at him again Brand threw up a protecting arm, blocking the fist aimed at his head. He let the man's momentum draw him in close, then sledged a hard fist of his own into the man's side, over the ribs, drawing a pained grunt. Brand hit him again in the same place. The man retreated, hurt, gasping for breath. Brand slammed the butt of the rifle's stock into his face. It tore through flesh to expose white bone that was suddenly awash with blood.

Turning Brand took long strides along the passage, coming to where Rimbaund was still trying to unlock Wyatt's cell. He whacked the rifle barrel across Rimbaund's ribs. The blow spun Rimbaund across the passage. He stumbled as he hit the wall, turning on Brand with an angry snarl. He went for his holstered gun. Brand was too close to use the rifle again so he dropped it, lunging at the big cowhand, his hands grabbing for Rimbaund's gun. Rimbaund swept his free hand round and clouted Brand across the mouth, splitting his lips. He looped his arm around Brand's neck, drawing it tight like a noose, crushing Brand against his thick chest. In seconds Brand felt his head spin as Rimbaund cut off his air supply. There was a heavy pounding behind his eyes, sweat popping out across his face. He knew he had to do something fast. While he still had the strength. With little conscious thought about it Brand threw his arm around Rimbaund's waist and lifted the man clear off the floor. He arched his body and launched himself across the passage, slamming Rimbaund against the bars of Wyatt's cell. Rimbaund's skull smashed hard against the iron bars. He grunted with pain and Brand felt the grip on his throat lessen. Reaching down Brand snatched out his Colt and whipped it across Rimbaund's head. The big cowman went down like a felled tree.

Taking the keys from the lock of Wyatt's cell Brand ran back into the office. He still had the Colt in his hand as he stepped from the jail and faced the group of men coming across the street. More of Rimbaund's crew. Probably the same men who had pursued him down the alley. Now they were coming to finish the job. Brand stepped to the edge of the boardwalk, letting them see the now-cocked Colt in his hand. When the group saw him they stopped. His appearance held them for that brief moment. His face was battered and bloody. Somewhere along the way his shirt had been torn and it was spattered with blood. More than any of those things was the terrible anger that showed in his eyes. And his voice when he spoke told them they were facing a man prepared to kill to maintain the order his job demanded.

"This is as far as you go!" Brand said. "Any man who wants to die just has to keep coming."

"Where's Rimbaund?"

"Right now he's out cold on the cell block floor. Damn lucky he isn't in a cell, or even dead. You want to join him?"

One of the group laughed harshly, still unconvinced.

"Step aside, Brand. We aim to take Rimbaund home." He took a step forward, making the mistake of letting his right hand drop close to the butt of the gun on his hip.

Brand's Colt only moved slightly. He touched the trigger and the weapon fired. The bullet caught the agitator in the right thigh, the force of the big .45 calibre bullet spinning him round and dumping him face down in the dirt.

"Now the rest of you get rid of your weapons. Now!" Brand ordered. After the group had obeyed Brand gestured towards the jail. "Now go and pick up your friends."

He followed them inside, keeping a close eye on them as they carried out the men who had broken into the jail. Bart Rimbaund was the last to leave. He was still dazed, blood streaming down his face.

"Any other time you'd all be in those cells. Right now I don't have the time to bother with you. I've got two people hurt because of your damn foolishness. If I find they're badly injured I'll be coming for you. Now clear the street."

He watched them trail away, hoping he could stay on his feet until they were out of sight. He was starting to feel weak, his body aching. Now the wildness was ebbing away, the adrenalin settling, his flesh was reacting to the punishment it had received. Brand's mind was whirling with a dozen different thoughts. Things he had to do — starting with getting help for Rick and Abby.

6

"*THE man is an animal! Damn him!*"

Judge Rice stared around the wrecked office, anger showing on his face.

"He sure enough spoiled my evening," Brand muttered. He finally located an unbroken mug in the debris on the floor. Crossing to the stove he filled the mug with hot coffee, flinching as the liquid touched his sore lips.

"Rimbaund has gone too far this time," Rice added, calmer now. "Deliberately smashing his way into the jail. Attacking a deputy. I'll issue a warrant for his arrest in the morning."

"Do me a favour, Judge," Brand said quietly. "Let me sort out one mess before we jump right into another. I'm only on the payroll to see the Wyatt thing through. Way things are going that eight thousand is running out fast."

Rice chose to ignore the final remark. "Do you think Rimbaund will try again?"

Brand shrugged. "No way of knowing. Rimbaund acts on impulse. He might figure the game's getting too costly. On the other hand he could just be sitting out there, thinking it over, and getting madder by the minute. We'll get to know sooner or later."

There was a loud hammering on the repaired jail door.

"Who is it?" Brand asked.

"Alvin Ritchie. Open this damn door, Brand."

Brand glanced at Judge Rice.

"Your fat, argumentative friend. Head of the town council and it's own worst enemy. Rich. Powerful, and a pain in the collective butt."

"That's all I need," Brand scowled and unlocked the door.

Ritchie bulled his way into the office. "Rice, just what the hell is going on?

We voted to hire this man as Marshal. Not public executioner. Already tonight we've had men beaten. Others shot to death. This is supposed to be a civilised community."

"Appears there are some of your citizens who don't realise that," Brand said pointedly.

Ritchie turned on him, his flabby face darkening with rage. "*A goddamn gunslinger!* Eight thousand dollars we laid out for you. We wanted a lawman. All we've got is a witless, kill-crazy gunslinger. *US Marshal?* It doesn't take much figuring as to why they threw you out."

Brand reached and took hold of Ritchie's coat. He swung the fat man round and slammed him up against the wall. Ritchie's teeth snapped together under the impact. He found himself staring into Brand's cold, hard face, and for a fleeting moment he felt the clammy hand of death on his shoulder.

"You paid me to run this office,

Ritchie, and to maintain the law in this town. That's what I'm doing. Not looking for trouble. Tonight some of *your* citizens broke the door down and forced their way into the jail and tried to free my prisoner. They beat up and knifed Rick Lander. They also shot an innocent young woman who happened to get in their way. And they tried to kill me. I didn't ask for any of that to happen. Now maybe I missed something, Mr Ritchie, so you tell me — how should I have handled it?"

"I . . . I . . . " For once Alvin Ritchie was lost for words. He knew now that he had stepped very close to the mark, pushing Brand a little too far. To his credit he took it no further. He remained silent, and sweated heavily.

Brand suddenly released him. Ritchie almost fell to the floor. He hauled himself upright, adjusting his rumpled clothing. His face was ashen as he glanced across at Judge Rice. Rice offered no comfort.

"I asked you earlier, Ritchie, but this

time I'm telling you. Get out of this office and stay out until you're invited back."

Ritchie scuttled out gratefully. Brand slammed the door behind him.

"Hell, Judge, I feel a whole lot better now."

Rice smiled. "Watch out for him, Brand. Ritchie's the kind who doesn't take kindly to being humiliated. He'll likely go out and pay Rimbaund to shoot you now."

Brand shrugged. Ritchie didn't worry him in the slightest. What concerned him was the fact that the night was far from over. There was time yet for the Wyatt bunch to make a play. There was no way of knowing how close they were to town even.

"You want me to stay around and lend a hand?" Rice asked.

Brand looked across at him, realising the Judge wasn't fooling. He meant it.

"This isn't going to get any easier, Judge."

"Listen, my boy, I was wearing a badge before you were born. I haven't always been a revered Judge. I worked my way up to it. Did a spell as a deputy. Town marshal. County sheriff. Three years in the Arizona Rangers. So don't you look at me like I don't know what I'm talking about. I'm not so old I can't handle a gun. Or see what I'm shooting at."

"Judge, I wouldn't even think that," Brand grinned. "You're hired."

Rice got up. "Give me an hour. I'll see what I can do about getting us some additional help."

After the Judge had left the office Brand did what he could to straighten the place up. There wasn't much he could do about the dark, drying bloodstains on the floor. Rick Lander's blood. Seeing it brought the incident back in a heady rush. It seemed so damn long ago, yet little more than an hour had passed.

Brand slumped in the office chair, a fresh mug of coffee in his hand, wondering just what the rest of the night was going to bring. One thing he was certain of — there would be little in the way of sweetness and understanding from his fellow man.

7

"**M**UCH trouble in town," Silvano said. "Shooting. One, maybe two men dead."

They had ridden to within a mile of the town before calling a halt. Sutter, Billy Reece and Al Wyatt had hidden out in a dry wash while Silvano had slipped into town to have a look round. It was an easy task for the breed; Silvano was only seen when *he* wanted to be seen. With the inborn skill of his ancestors he had moved around Adobe, watching and listening until he had all the information he wanted, and had then slipped away from the town without being noticed.

"So what happened?" Sutter asked.

"In town I heard plenty of angry talk. There is a new marshal. They call him Brand — Jason Brand."

"Brand? Where the hell did they get

him from so damned fast?"

"He was in the jail," Silvano explained. "Too much drink so they lock him up. Now they have let him out and given him a badge."

"Ain't he the one used to be a US Marshal?" Billy Reece asked.

Sutter nodded. "That's him. Hard as they come and a mean hand with a gun. That town's on a winning streak."

"I heard lynch talk," Silvano said. "Men in saloon get whisky brave. Man called Brand killed one of them. They wait for dark then attack jail. Brand comes when they are inside jail. He fights like a wild one. No mercy. He kills with ease. Throws them all out of jail. He's a bad one, Sutter. He will not bend or break."

"*Shit!*" Sutter exploded. He was thinking about Ben Wyatt's feelings about things having gone wrong. *Christ, Ben, I'm beginning to believe you were right.*

"That son of a bitch is going to

have the jail closed up tighter than an old maid's drawers," Billy Reece said. "He won't be letting a damn thing get close."

"We've got to do something!"

Al Wyatt's voice broke the silence he'd held since Sutter had given him his beating. Al was a sore loser, in more ways than one, and he had retreated into a sullen silence. He looked as bad as he felt. His face was a battered, tender mass of bloody bruises.

"Not much time left to get to Ben," Silvano said.

Sutter glanced at him. "Meaning?"

"Adobe has own Judge. And court-house. They are going to hold trial. Talk says Ben will hang."

"No!" Al's protest was a shrill wail. "They ain't goin' to hang Ben! No way. If you bastards won't help I'll get him out myself."

"We'll help him, Al, and you damnwell know it!" Sutter stood up, his face angry. "So you quit that talk else I'll kick some more shit out of you.

The only way we can help Ben is to do some hard talking before we go back to Adobe."

"Talk! that's all you ever do," Al sneered. "I don't know why Ben ever let you ride with us."

He turned away into the darkness, and silence fell over the group.

"Jake?" Reece said.

"Let him alone," Sutter said. "I got enough to do without worrying about that little pissant."

They began to talk over the way they might get Ben Wyatt out of Adobe's jail. It was a few minutes later when they heard the sound of a horse being ridden away from the gully. Reece vanished into the shadows where the horses had been tethered. He was back moments later.

"It's Al. He's taken his horse and gone."

Silvano shook his dark head. "He will try to get Ben out himself."

"Hell, they'll hear him coming before he gets to town That boy couldn't tiptoe through a graveyard without he woke the dead. He'll foul it up for us, Jake."

"Maybe not," Sutter mused. "He'll more than likely get himself killed. Brand can take someone like Al in his sleep. I hope he blows a hole right through the little asshole. It'll save me the trouble."

There was no argument from either Silvano or Billy Reece. Both of them had suffered under Al Wyatt. Before there had always been Ben ready to defend Al's behaviour. But this time Ben wasn't around, and no one else was about to put their life on the line for Al Wyatt. Al was undoubtedly riding into Adobe to stop a bullet. They all knew but Al himself.

★ ★ ★

The thought he might be in danger never once crossed Al Wyatt's mind. Deep thinking wasn't one of his talents. As long as Ben was around

Al had never needed to do anything but take orders. He thought as he acted — like a spoiled child, and Ben Wyatt, prompted by a lifetime of looking out for his younger brother, always made Al's decisions for him.

One thing *had* stuck in Al's mind. Silvano had spoken about Adobe having its own Judge, and he would preside over Ben's trial. For once in his life Al produced a clear, to him, line of thought. *If there was no Judge there couldn't be a trial.* Al knew that another Judge would be sent for. It would take time and that extra time would give them a better chance to free Ben from jail.

Al lashed his horse viciously, spurring it along the trail to Adobe. The more he thought about his plan the better he liked it. Ben would be proud of him. The solution was so damn simple.

Kill the Judge and stop the trial!

Al laughed wildly, the shrill sound whipped away by the wind.

He slowed his horse as he made out

the dark outline of the town ahead. He took the animal in as close as he dared, then dismounted and tethered it in a thicket. He made his way to the outskirts on foot, finding himself at the poorer end of town. Here there was a collection of shacks and adobes, all in a poor state of repair. It was said you could find a whore who would only charge fifty-cents; maybe, Al thought, he might find a man who would kill for that amount. He giggled at his own joke.

He skirted the dark fringes of Adobe, moving up towards the residential area. He was still a distance away when he stopped, slipping into the shadows as a curse bubbled from his lips. Something had just come to him. Something he hadn't given thought to. He didn't know where the Judge lived. How could he kill the man if he wasn't able to find him? He couldn't go round knocking on doors until he found the right house. But he had to find out somehow.

100

He heard the man before he saw him. A mumbling, shambling figure who appeared out of the shadows. Al saw a thin, hunched body. A battered, greasy hat pulled down over a gaunt face. Filthy, bone thin hands clutching a tattered coat around an emaciated form. In the thin light the man's face showed sickly white. "Hey, mister, got the price of a drink?" Even the voice was thin, all the spirit gone from it. "Just a few cents, mister, for a veteran of the War Between the States."

Al giggled softly to himself. A veteran! The war had been over for twenty years, but here was this drunk still trading on past glories. He was about to shove the man aside when he realised he could use him.

"How'd you like to be able to buy a couple of bottles? The best whisky in town?" Al pulled money from his pocket.

The man's bloodshot eyes, dark-ringed and watery, gleamed with anticipation.

101

He held out a clawing hand.

"I need something first," Al said, drawing the money away.

"Have a heart, mister. I need a drink bad. My guts're all twisted up."

"Do what I want and you can drink yourself all to hell."

"So what is it?" the man asked sullenly.

"I need to see the Judge real bad. But I only just got to town. You know where he lives?"

"Him?" The man spat. "Sure I know. It's at the other end of town. Hell of a walk though."

"Take me there."

"Jesus Christ! I don't like that son of a bitch. Every time I get drunk he throws me in jail. I don't know . . . "

Al shrugged. He began to pocket the money.

"All I need is for you to show me his house. I ain't asking' you to set the place on fire. If you don't want the money forget it. I'll find somebody else."

The man sighed, grumbled under his sour breath. Then: "Aw, hell, I'll do it." His desire for a drink finally overcame his distaste for actually having to work for it. "C'mon."

He led Al through town by a devious route along backlots and down alleys. Al didn't complain. He wanted secrecy.

"Here we are, mister."

They were in a narrow alley. The drunk was pointing across the street at a neat, white-painted house. A lamp shone in a downstairs window.

"That there is Judge Rice's place." The boney fingers plucked at Al's sleeve. "What about my money, mister? You said you'd give it to me."

Al grinned out of the darkness. "Sure," he said. "*Here!*"

Cold light glinted on the blade of Al's knife as it flashed out of the shadows and into the drunk's throat. A rattling gasp bubbled from the man's lips and red froth began to stain his teeth. Al shoved hard on the knife, working the blade from side to side, opening a ragged, bloody wound. The drunk's body twitched violently as he tried to dislodge the heavy blade buried in his flesh. It was useless. Al had him pinned against the wall and he held the frail body there until all movement had ceased. When the man stopped moving Al jerked the knife free and let the limp form drop to the ground. Wiping the blade down his pants Al turned back towards the street.

And froze.

A man had stepped out of the Judge's house. A slight, white haired man dressed in black. He had a rolled bundle under one arm and a sheaf of papers in his hand. Al saw that the light had gone out in the window of the house. This had to be the Judge. Al watched him walk briskly along the street. He was heading for the centre of town.

The jail! He was going to the jail.

Once he was inside Al's chance to kill him would lessen.

Slipping out of the alley Al followed

the Judge. He eased his gun from its holster and dogged back the hammer. The street was deserted at the moment. Al hurried to get closer to the Judge. He was only going to get one chance, so he couldn't afford to fail. Ben was depending on him.

Thin shafts of moonlight broke through the heavy clouds. From the saloons came the babble of voices. From opposite establishments the jangle of tuneless pianos met with a jarring noise. At a hitching rail a restless horse snorted, raising dust from the street.

Still trailing the Judge Al suddenly realised he was closer to the jail than he wanted to be. He was going to have to make his move now.

He lifted the heavy Colt, levelling it at the Judge's slim back.

"Hey, boy, what you doin'?"

The voice was deep and drink-slurred. It sounded loud on the empty street. Panic rose in Al. He turned and saw a rawboned cowboy peering at him from the boardwalk, only yards away.

Clutching a bottle in one scarred hand, the cowboy was the worse for wear — but he was still capable of figuring out what Al was doing.

Al's gun boomed, throwing out a vivid lash of flame. The cowboy was slammed back across the boardwalk, pawing at the bloody wound in his chest. The moment he had fired Al turned his attention back to the Judge. Rice was running for the jail.

No, Al cursed, *you won't run out on me*.

He followed the Judge, throwing up the Colt. He touched the trigger and felt the gun jump in his fist. Saw the bullet rip through the Judge's shoulder. Rice stumbled, dropping his belongings. He managed to stay on his feet. Kept running, awkwardly now. The jail was closer. Al's anger spurred him on. He wasn't going to quit now. Not now he was so close . . . he cocked the gun and fired again. This time the Judge went down, skidding along the ground on his face. Al laughed, his elation running high.

Got the bastard!

The excitement was too much for him and he threw caution aside. He hooted wildly, the sound filling the night air.

"Hey, Ben, I got the damn Judge off your back!"

The jail door burst open and a tall figure stepped out onto the boardwalk. Al caught sight of the badge on the man's vest.

The man himself! Marshal Jason Brand!

Al sniggered to himself. Maybe he wouldn't look so damn big with a .45 bullet in him. He swung the Colt up and round, bringing the hammer back.

He saw the tall figure move. A blur of action. Then a gun fired, the sound filling the street. Al felt a heavy blow strike his chest. He tried to scream but there was no sound left in him. He saw Brand's gun blossom flame again and this time there was a sharp, terrible pain. He was on the ground, staring up at the sky. There was a roaring in his ears. His limbs felt leaden. So heavy he couldn't move. His body began to tremble violently from the shock. He tried to speak again. All that happened was a gush of blood from his mouth.

Christ it was hurting . . . Ben . . . Ben where are you?

Al flopped over on his side. When he looked down he could see the blood pumping out of the ragged holes in his chest.

Hell Ben I nearly did it!

He began to cough. The sound was ragged and it brought a fresh surge of pain that overwhelmed him. It grew and smothered him, blotting out everything else, and when the pain faded Al Wyatt was dead.

8

AL WYATT'S second bullet had struck Judge Rice in the back, passing close to the heart on its way through his body. Rice had lost a lot of blood during the operation to repair the damage. Adobe's doctor, Sam Elliot, did what he could, admitting all the time that Rice was injured badly, and knowing it would be a miracle if the Judge survived. Rice became weaker by the minute. Elliot passed the news to Brand when he called in at the jail sometime later.

"Will he live?"

Elliot peered over the top of his steel-rimmed spectacles at Adobe's temporary lawman.

"Hard to say. He's an old man, but he's tough. Losing all that blood isn't going to make it any easier."

"Damn!" Brand paced the office,

deep in thought. He had almost forgotten the doctor was with him.

"You thinking about the trial?" Elliot asked.

"Has to be faced. With the Judge out of action there isn't going to be a trial."

"No more circuit Judge in this area. Since Caleb took over permanently the circuit rider doesn't cover this part of the territory any more. We could ask for a replacement. Take time though." Elliot focussed on Brand. "That, I take it, is something we don't have?"

"You said it, doc." Brand paused in front of the office window. He was silent for a while, then he snapped back into action, his decision reached. "There is a way out."

"What?"

"Get Wyatt out of town. Somewhere a trial can be held. It would take the pressure off Adobe as well."

"I guess you're right on that at least. The longer Wyatt's in town the more likely we are to have trouble."

"I don't need any more problems. Tonight's been enough. Any minute now Ritchie is going to come storming back in here."

"He worry you?" Elliot asked.

Brand shook his head. "He's just a damn nuisance. What I'm more concerned about is the wrong people getting hurt if things blow up again."

"What do you plan for Wyatt?"

Brand crossed to the large map of the territory pinned to the wall behind the desk. He jabbed a finger at Adobe's location.

"Here we are. Two days away is Yuma. They've got a good lawforce there. Plus a Judge and a courthouse. Something else too. Yuma Pen. Once Ben Wyatt is behind those walls his bunch can kiss him goodbye. He can stay there until the trial is set."

"Makes sense," Elliot agreed. "But it's a long ride to Yuma. Rough country too. A man alone, with a prisoner in tow as well, would be pretty fair game for the likes of Wyatt's bunch."

"Doc, I'm not wild about the idea myself. It just seems a better deal than sitting inside this jail waiting for something to happen. Bart Rimbaund is still out there. Add him to Wyatt's bunch and we've got trouble from two directions. Sooner or later this town is going to bust wide open. I'll take my chances out in the open."

Elliot nodded in understanding.

There was a firm knock at the door. Brand picked up his rifle, waving Elliot aside.

"Yeah?"

"Clem Bishop, Brand. And a couple of others. Judge asked us to lend a hand."

"That's Clem all right," Elliot said.

Brand opened the door and allowed the three men to step inside.

"The Judge came to see us before he got shot. Said you needed a few extra guns," Clem Bishop said. He was a capable looking man in his late thirties. The hand he held out to Brand was big and workscarred.

"This here is Vic Brown and Joe Meacher."

"You want to take a break, Marshal, you go right ahead," Bishop said. "Ain't no way anyone will get through that door lessen we let them."

Brand smiled. "I could have done with you boys a while back."

"Way I heard it the other side needed the help."

"I don't figure to make a habit of that kind of thing," Brand said. "Anyway I aim to take Wyatt out of town come morning. Ride him over to Yuma and let the law there deal with him."

"Then you need some rest," Meacher said. "Go on, get out of here, Marshal. You ain't wanted until morning. Ben Wyatt will be ready when you need him."

"Thanks." Brand indicated the rack of guns on the wall. "Help yourselves to the rifles. Plenty of ammunition there too."

"Is there plenty of coffee?" Brown

asked. "That's all I need."

"Full pot on the stove. Plenty of makings in the cupboard there."

"Doc, get him out of here. He looks ready to fall down."

"I thought he looked pretty good after my patching up," Elliot said.

"I seen pots of stewed beef that looked better," Vic Brown said dryly.

"Come on, Brand, let's leave these roughnecks alone."

They left the jail. The door closed behind them with a solid thump. Brand heard the bolt slide into place and the lock click.

"Keep me in touch with the Judge's condition," Brand said.

Elliot nodded. "Will do. By the way, I have a message for you. There's a young woman been asking after you. It appears she's becoming worried because you haven't been to see her."

"How is Abby?"

"Fine now," Elliot said. "She was lucky though. That bullet only burned her arm. I think a visit from you would cheer her up."

They parted company there on the street, Elliot heading back for his office. Brand continued along the street, crossing when he neared the residential area. Abby lived in a small, comfortable house that had belonged to her aunt, the woman who had brought Abby up since the death of her parents when she had still been a child. The aunt herself had died a few years back, leaving Abby the house and her savings.

Brand walked up the narrow path leading from the gate to the house. There was a lamp glowing softly behind drawn curtains in the front room. He stepped up on the porch and tapped on the door.

"Yes?" Abby's voice asked after a minute.

"Jason Brand."

The door opened and Abby stood there, soft lit from the hall lamp. Her face was radiant, thick hair down and loose on her shoulders. She was wearing a soft, clinging robe.

"I was hoping you might call," she said, reaching out to take his arm and usher him inside.

As he stood there he heard the door close, and caught the soft click of the key turning in the lock.

"Is there any news about Rick or the Judge?"

"The Judge is in a bad way. Right now the doc can't say if he'll pull through or not. All we can do is wait. Pretty much the same with Rick. That knife he took cut him up badly inside. He'll pull through or die. Simple as that, and there isn't a damn thing we can do about it."

"I'm sorry, Jason. It can't be easy for you."

"Me? Hell, girl I'm fine. All I got were a few more bruises. I'll mend. They might not be so lucky."

"You look tired," Abby said. She led him into the living room and pushed him down on a soft couch. "I'll bring you some coffee."

Brand leaned back and tried to relax. The couch was comfortable. He dropped his hat on the carpet by the couch and closed his eyes. Adding everything up it had been one hell of a day. There was no denying that.

One hell of a day!

"Coffee."

Brand opened his eyes. Abby was bending over him. She was holding out a cup. He could smell the rich aroma of hot coffee. He took the cup. The coffee tasted good.

"What are you going to do now Judge Rice is hurt?"

Brand lowered the cup. "I'm taking Wyatt over to Yuma in the morning. Let the law there handle his trial."

"But what about Wyatt's men? You can't just ride out of town knowing they're out there somewhere."

"If I stay there'll only be more trouble in Adobe. I don't want anyone else getting hurt."

Abby stared at him, her face creased by a frown.

"And you'll do it, won't you? Risk your own life taking Ben Wyatt to Yuma. With those outlaws just waiting to get you on your own. For heaven's sake, Jason Brand, why? Why risk your life for this town? You don't even know it,"

"I took its money, Abby. I agreed to do a job. And that job isn't over until Ben Wyatt is delivered to Yuma."

Abby sighed. "Oh well, I suppose you know what you're doing." She sat on the couch beside him. "Will you be coming back to Adobe?"

"I don't know."

"At least you're honest. In that case we have some unfinished business of our own to take care of."

"We do?"

"Oh yes," she said. "The last time we were together somebody decided to start shooting at us. Remember?"

"Only dimly."

"It wasn't all that long ago."

"Yeah, but I've had a busy night."

Abby laughed softly. "Mister Brand, it isn't over yet."

"What about your arm?"

"I thought you'd never ask. Do you want to see the scar?"

"You mean it's healed already?"

"It's feeling much better now you're here."

Abby loosened her robe and let it fall open. She eased it from her shoulder, exposing her arm.

"Neat bandage," Brand observed, not really giving a damn about her arm.

Abby kissed him gently, her mouth soft and warm. She stirred restlessly as Brand slid his hands across her bared body.

"That is not my wounded arm, Mister Brand."

"Who cares, Miss Abby."

Abby sighed. "Well I don't for one. One thing, though."

"Yeah?"

"Just for tonight — take off that

damn gun and leave it next to your boots."

"I haven't taken my boots off," he said.

"*Not yet you haven't.*"

9

BRAND left Abby still sleeping. He had eased out of bed, dressed and had left the house to make his way through the early morning calm to Doc Elliot's office. A lamp still burned on Elliot's desk. Brand opened the door and went in.

"Doc? You there?"

Elliot appeared. He looked haggard and unshaven. Pulling on his spectacles he nodded in recognition.

"Coffee?"

"Thanks, doc."

Elliot brought two filled mugs across, handing one to Brand.

"What's the news?"

Elliot shook his head. "Not too good. Rick died a half hour ago."

"Damn." Brand stared into his mug of coffee. "He was a good kid. What about Rice?"

121

"Slightly better," Elliot said. "I think he's going to make it. Be a long haul. He isn't a young man any more."

"None of us are, doc."

"Just one thing, Brand. Rick spoke to me shortly before he died. He told me who knifed him. It was Bart Rimbaund."

"Wouldn't you know it," Brand said icily.

He left Elliot's office a few minutes later. Before he went to the jail there was something he had to do. The death of Rick Lander meant he had to bring in Bart Rimbaund on a murder charge. It was the least he could do for the young deputy. He hadn't known Rick for long, and their relationship hadn't exactly been a cordial one. But Jason Brand had recognised the fire driving the young lawman. He had also seen a lot of himself in Rick and there had been a trace of envy in that observation. Not that there was need for envy now. Rick Lander was dead,

by a sheet in Elliot's back
d for what? So that a bunch
en cowhands could release
it up brutality in a savage
spree of violence? It was too much
of a waste. Too much to allow it to
go unpunished.

Brand made his way to the Adobe
Palace. He pulled his Colt and made
sure it was fully loaded.

Here we go again, he told himself
wearily. One day he was going to
walk into one of these situations and
it would be his turn to be carried
out feet first. It had to happen. By
the law of averages his day had to
come. The day when he faced a gun
just a shade faster. A touch surer.
He couldn't go on bucking the odds
forever. Sooner or later he was going
to catch the bullet with his name on
it.

He stopped short of the Palace.
There was someone on the boardwalk.
Brand recognised the owner of the
saloon. Phil Hoyt.

"Morning, Marshal," Hoyt said. early isn't it? Or is this in the line duty?"

"It's business," Brand admitted. "Is Rimbaund still inside?"

"No. Him and his crew left a few minutes ago. Headed for the corrals yonder." Hoyt jerked a finger in the direction of the distant livery.

"Thanks."

"Marshal?"

"Yeah?"

Hoyt stepped down off the boardwalk. "You going after Rimbaund?"

Brand nodded. "Rick Lander just died. He identified Rimbaund as the man who knifed him."

"I knew that son of a bitch would do it one day. He should have been put down years ago."

"He'll be out of your hair after today."

"Marshal, if you intend taking Rimbaund in — be careful. Don't give him an edge. Don't trust anything he says or does."

124

"I don't intend to, Hoyt, but thanks for the advice."

★ ★ ★

The corrals were near the burned out livery the Wyatt bunch had set to draw the town away from the bank.

Bart Rimbaund and his crew were in one of the corrals, saddling their horses. They were all so busy none of them saw or heard Brand approach, or even move to stand at the open gate of the corral.

Rimbaund himself was the first to see Brand. He had walked to the gate to pick up the saddle he'd left there, and the first indication of Brand's presence was the muzzle of the big Colt that suddenly appeared and centered on Rimbaund's face.

"Gun on the ground," Brand said evenly. "Make one false move and I'll spread your brains across this corral."

Rimbaund sensed the threat behind Brand's words, and for once in his life he used good judgement. Unbuckling his belt he let the gunrig slip to the ground.

"Now step out here," Brand said.

"What is this?" Rimbaund asked.

"You're under arrest, Rimbaund.

"*Arrest!*" Rimbaund laughed. "What the hell for?"

"The murder of Rick Lander. Remember. He was a deputy. A lawman. And you killed him, Rimbaund."

"Little pissant."

"He pointed the finger at you before he died. Told Doc Elliot."

"You can't just . . . "

"Rimbaund, whatever way you call it the name is murder. You killed Rick Lander . . . now you pay. Like you expect Ben Wyatt to pay."

Rage flared in Rimbaund's eyes. He lunged forward, massive hands snatching for Brand's gun. Brand stepped aside, and as Rimbaund came in range he whipped the barrel of his Colt down across the cowboy's skull. He struck a couple more times before

Rimbaund went down.

"Hey! What the hell's goin' on?"

The shout drew Brand's attention. He looked up and saw one of Rimbaund's partners running across the corral. The man had his gun out, and as Brand spotted him the gun snapped up and fired. The bullet whacked into the corral post inches from Brand's face, filling the air with ragged splinters of wood. Brand dropped to a crouch, leaning to one side of the post. His Colt came up, levelled, and returned fire. His shot took the man in the left shoulder. A gout of blood misted the air, the force of the .45 calibre bullet dropping the wounded man in the churned up corral dirt.

"On your feet, Rimbaund," Brand yelled. He took hold of Rimbaund's shirt and hauled him upright. The big cowboy, still dazed, offered no resistance. "Let's go. Head for the jail. Any of your partners try to stop us I'll put a bullet through your spine and worry about it later." Brand jabbed the Colt's muzzle in Rimbaund's back. "Tell 'em, Rimbaund, and make 'em believe it. If they don't I promise you'll be the first to go."

Rimbaund swore in frustration. He was tied hand and foot, and even Bart Rimbaund had to admit that.

"Back off, boys. He's got the drop on me. Leave it for now and wait your chance."

There was no opposition from the men gathered in the corral. Brand turned Rimbaund away and walked him directly to the jail. He hammered on the door, identifying himself to the men inside. The door finally opened and Brand shoved Rimbaund inside.

"Morning, Marshal," Clem Bishop said. He glanced at Rimbaund. "He just paying a call or does he need a room?"

"He's staying."

Rimbaund was escorted through to the cells.

"Why?" Clem Bishop asked.

"Rick Lander died a while ago. It

was Rimbaund who knifed him. So he goes to Yuma with Wyatt."

"Can't say as how I'll miss Rimbaund," Bishop said. "Always was a miserable feller."

"Yeah?" Brand perched himself on the edge of the desk with a mug of coffee. "Well he'll be able to find out just how tough he is when they toss him in Yuma Pen."

"Marshal, do you want me or any of the boys to ride over with you?"

Brand shook his head. "I appreciate the offer, Clem, but I don't want anyone else getting hurt. I'm paid to do the job. It's my profession. Not yours. Thanks, but no thanks."

"We'll stay on here until you ride out," Bishop said. "By the way did I hear a couple of shots a while back?"

"One of Rimbaund's boys figured to stop me taking him away. He didn't have the talent to match his idea. He'll have a sore shoulder to remind him how stupid he was."

"I'll say one thing, Brand. Adobe is

going to be a quiet town after you've gone."

"*Amen to that*," Brand said.

★ ★ ★

An hour later Brand had horses and supplies ready for the ride to Yuma. He had picked a cutdown shotgun in addition to his rifle and handgun. Each weapon had been stripped down, cleaned and reassembled. Extra ammunition had been packed in his saddlebags.

He decided to ride out before the sun rose too high. It was going to be a hot day. Brand was standing outside the jail after checking the horses when he became aware of someone watching him. It was Abby. He crossed the street to meet her.

"You ran out on me," she said.

"After last night there was no chance of me *running* anywhere," he told her. "And there wasn't any point waking you."

"Oh?" Abby smiled boldy. "You

seemed to want me awake last night. Most of the night as I recall."

"Abby, it was good. For both of us after everything we'd been through."

Her smile faded. "Is that all it was, Jason? Just something to make us forget a bad day?"

"Maybe a little more than that."

"Only a little?"

"Abby . . ."

"No . . . I . . . damn you!" she said angrily. "It's always the same isn't it? Don't you ever think it might mean just that much more to a woman? Maybe for me it was a beginning. The start of something to . . ."

"No, Abby, not with me. Not with the way I live. I can't afford to get involved. I don't even know if I'll be back this way after I've delivered Wyatt to Yuma. It's the way I am, Abby. I don't settle. I don't build relationships. Not any more. I did once and someone I cared for paid a terrible price. So I don't let it happen. It's always the good people around me who end up paying."

Abby searched his face, reaching out to touch his arm. "I guess I should have known. You said last night you might not come back. And you haven't made me any promises." She looked at him with a wistful expression in her eyes. "I won't make a fuss, Jason Brand. But try not to forget me. And if you do come by this way again . . . "

"You'll be the first to know," he said.

She glanced across at the waiting horses — then back at Brand. "Be careful," she said. She kissed him. Quickly. Then turned her face away so he couldn't see the tears.

Brand watched her turn and vanish inside the restaurant. He crossed the street. Reaching the jail he stepped up on the boardwalk. He saw a bunch of riders approaching.

It was Rimbaund's crew.

He stayed where he was, waiting for them. As they drew level with the jail the riders reined in.

"We're leaving town, Marshal," one of them said.

"I won't argue with that."

"Things kind of got out hand. Bart, he shouldn't have done what he did. Rick Lander . . . it ain't right he died. Not that way. You won't have any more trouble from us, Marshal, and we apologise for what happened."

Brand nodded briefly. He watched the riders move on along the street, glad that a confrontation had been avoided. The riders drifted out of sight at the far end of town.

Doc Elliot came out of his office and walked down to the jail.

"I just attended to another customer," he said. "If I was that way inclined I could say you were good for business."

Brand smiled dryly, turned and went inside the jail with Elliot behind him.

"I hear you have Bart Rimbaund behind bars," Elliot said.

"He'll be company for Wyatt on the ride to Yuma."

Clem Bishop said: "Doc, we offered

to ride with the Marshal to Yuma."

"Brand?"

"Look, doc, with Wyatt's boys waiting out there I can't afford to be worrying about other people," Brand explained. "Like I told Clem, the offer's appreciated, but I work better on my own."

"I really hope you make it," Bishop said.

"*Well that makes two of us!*" Brand said.

He went to the desk and opened a drawer. From its depths he dragged out a set of manacles.

"Time we got this party on the road."

He opened the door to the cells, taking the keys from their peg on the wall, and made his way down to where Wyatt and Rimbaund were waiting.

He noted Wyatt's moody silence the moment he reached the outlaw's cell. There was something on the man's mind. He would bear watching closely,

Brand decided. He had a feeling it had started when he'd told Wyatt about Al's death and his own involvement in it. Wyatt wasn't giving too much away right now, but he wasn't a man who would forget such a thing.

Brand unlocked both cells, then stepped back from the doors. He made sure both men could see the gun he held in his right hand.

"Step out, boys, but do it easy. It was a hard day yesterday and today looks like being the same. So don't push me."

Wyatt simply stared at him, his drawn face pale. The scar he wore down one cheek flared red. He walked from the cell and stood watching Brand.

"Maybe I'll just stay where I am," Rimbaund said.

"You step out here, mister, and be damn quick about it!" Brand swung the Colt to cover the big cowboy. "I can still finish what I started back out by the corral."

"Shoot me? Here in front of all these witnesses? Even you won't do that, Brand."

"You really want to try me, Rimbaund?"

Rimbaund held his gaze for a moment. Then he made an angry sound deep in his throat. "The hell with you." He stepped out of the cell to stand next to Wyatt.

Brand tossed the set of manacles to Wyatt.

"Fasten one to your right wrist."

Wyatt held the manacles and stared at them. It seemed he might refuse. But he finally placed the metal band around his wrist and closed the open end. Brand passed him the key and watched him lock it.

"Now put the other on Rimbaund's left wrist."

Rimbaund made a growl of protest. "Hell, no! You ain't chaining me to that . . ."

Brand hit him. There was no warning. He simply leaned forward and slugged Rimbaund in the mouth. The blow knocked Rimbaund into the iron bars of the cell. Blood burst from a cut lip.

"Do it, Wyatt."

"Maybe I don't want him chained to me."

"Wyatt, neither of you has a choice in the matter. Do it my way or I'll haul you to Yuma with a bullet through your knee."

Wyatt backed off. He knew Brand wasn't making idle threats. He meant every word he said. The outlaw wasn't going to risk getting hurt. If a chance to escape arose Wyatt wanted to be able to take it.

Brand watched as Wyatt locked the other end of the manacles on Rimbaund's wrist. Then he took the key back.

"No man ever put a chain on me before," Rimbaund growled. "I won't forget it, Brand."

"I'll try to live with that," Brand said. He pointed in the direction of the office. "Coffee in there. Get what you can because it might be a while before there's any more available."

Wyatt and Rimbaund made their way through to the office, crossing to the stove where the coffee pot bubbled on the heat. They each filled a mug and drank.

"What about some food?" Rimbaund demanded.

"If I decide to give it."

"*Bastard!*" Rimbaund turned angrily, his action jerking Wyatt off balance and spilling the outlaw's hot coffee down his shirt.

Wyatt reacted swiftly. He dropped his own mug, then caught hold of Rimbaund's shirt, pulling him close.

"Cowboy, I might be stuck with you, but go easy or I'll beat your damn head clean off your shoulders."

The threat did little to deter Rimbaund. He simply tossed the contents of his mug into Wyatt's face. Wyatt yelled in pain. He slammed a big shoulder into Rimbaund's chest, driving him across the floor and up against the wall. His face creasing in agony Rimbaund drove his knee into Wyatt's stomach. Wyatt staggered back, sucking in air. Rimbaund's free hand lashed out, catching Wyatt across the side of the head. The blow made Wyatt stumble, then found he was being brought up short by the chain that connected him to the other man. It made it hard to avoid being hit. Despite this the pair went at it with a vengeance, battering each other with open hostility until Brand stepped in and separated them. "Keep this up and I'll end up burying the pair of you in Adobe."

"Then tell this cowboy to back off," Wyatt yelled, spitting blood.

"You two are going to have to live together until we reach Yuma," Brand told them. "One of you dies the other's going to have to carry him."

Rimbaund growled, jerking the chain that tied him to Wyatt.

"You want them mounted up?" Clem Bishop asked.

Brand nodded. Bishop and his partners ushered the scowling prisoners out of the jail.

Doc Elliot said: "You watch yourself out there."

"Do my best, doc. Pull the Judge through if you can."

"I have a feeling he'll do it all by himself," Elliot smiled.

Brand stepped outside. A crowd was gathering, watching in silence. He climbed onto his own horse and took up the reins. He held them in his left hand. The shotgun was in his right, the butt of the stock nestled against his hip.

"Let's go," he said, letting Wyatt and Rimbaund ride just ahead of him. "Thanks for the help, fellers," he said to Elliot and Bishop, and then the jail fell behind him. The main street took them out of Adobe. The open plain stretched before them, wide and desolate, and apparently deserted. Brand knew better than that.

He began to get the feeling it was going to be a long ride to Yuma. He *knew* it would be far from being a peaceful trip.

10

WHEN Billy Reece rolled out of his blanket in the chill light of dawn he imagined he was the first. Then he found the fire burning brightly and a pot of coffee bubbling over the flames.

Silvano!

Reece grinned. The breed was usually up and about before first light. He poured himself some coffee and settled back on his heels. A few minutes later Jake Sutter joined him, stretching his lean body. Sutter remained silent until he swallowed a mug of the coffee.

"Silvano back out again?" he asked.

"Reckon," Reece said. "Made up the fire and took himself off by the looks of it." He moved to prepare breakfast.

Sutter sat and watched him.

"Jake, what do you reckon's happened to Al?" Reece asked finally, unable to curb his curiosity.

"I *hope* Brand had the good sense to shoot him."

"Could turn out the other way."

"Only if Jason Brand was deaf, dumb and blind last night. There's no other way Al could take him. Little prick hardly knows one end of a gun from the other."

"Al is dead!"

Reece glanced up and saw that Silvano was squatting on his heels on the other side of the cookfire.

"Wish you'd quit doin' that," he complained. "Sneakin' up on folk."

"What happened?" Sutter asked.

"Al went after Judge. Shot him up pretty bad. Story goes that Brand shot Al. Judge still lives — but Al is dead."

"I always did like a story with a happy ending," Sutter said. He caught Silvano's eye. "What's happening now?"

"Talk is that Brand will take Ben to Yuma to stand trial. He will be put in Yuma Pen until court is ready. Brand will take other man. Called Rimbaund.

The one who killed the young deputy guarding the jail."

"Jake, if we want Ben we'll need to get to him before Yuma," Reece said.

"We will," Sutter told him. "Brand's making it easy for us. If he's riding to Yuma we can trail him, pick our spot and do it without half of Adobe on our backs."

"That easy?"

Sutter shook his head. "Didn't say it was going to be easy. But we'll have a damn sight better chance out here."

They ate breakfast. Silvano finished first. He picked up his rifle and stood up.

"I go watch for Brand. Mark his trail for you to follow."

Sutter nodded. "We'll be ready."

Silvano vanished from sight, the only mark of his passing a thin mist of dust hanging in the air.

Sutter and Reece finished eating. They broke camp, taking their time, confident in Silvano's ability to spot and track Brand and his prisoners.

They packed away their gear, checking the horses thoroughly. The sun had risen by the time they were ready to move out, burning away the last remnants of the night's chill.

They rode out, following the trail Silvano had left for them. For a half hour they rode in silence, watching the land around them. Even so Silvano rode in from behind them, coming alongside almost before they spotted him.

"He has left Adobe. With Ben and the man called Rimbaund. They ride west for Yuma."

Sutter eased his butt in the saddle, smiling thinly

"Let's get to it," he said.

★ ★ ★

Brand rode with the knowledge that his two prisoners, though manacled, were far from finished. Neither of them was about to take the trip to Yuma without putting up some kind of resistance.

145

Given the slightest opportunity Wyatt or Rimbaund would kill him without a moment's hesitation.

Brand didn't allow any of his thoughts to cloud his judgement of the situation. He was aware that Wyatt's partners were somewhere close by. He hadn't seen them yet — but he knew they were around.

The morning slid by with agonising slowness. The heat bore down on them with a physical force. There was no avoiding it. Brand called a halt around midmorning so they could take a drink. Rimbaund started to complain about food again, and as before Brand ignored him.

Noon came and went. Brand still hadn't picked up any sign. It looked as if Wyatt's partners were biding their time. Giving Brand a chance to get well clear of Adobe before they played their hand.

Mid afternoon. Dust rose in stinging clouds. It clung to them. The sun was still hot. Brand's shirt clung damply to his back and he was stiff from long hours in the saddle. His senses stayed razor-sharp and his concentration hadn't wavered. He knew the penalty for losing the edge. Out here the first chance was the only chance. After that it didn't matter what happened. A dead man tended to lose interest fast.

He spotted the three riders as they came slowly down a long ridge off to the south. At the back of his mind he had held the suspicion that Wyatt's partners had been watching him from the high ground. He was being proved right. They had probably been with him from the minute he'd left Adobe. Actually seeing them eased the tension.

He kept the riders in view as they continued their distant trailing. They seemed content to stay well away for the moment. At the same time they were letting him know they were around. In no hurry. Then why should they hurry? They had him where they wanted him, and all they needed to do was pick the time and the place to suit themselves.

All *he* could do was to be ready when they did make their move.

★ ★ ★

When Sutter led off the ridge they knew Brand had spotted them. Not that it mattered. There was no place for him to run. So they simply trailed him, keeping him in sight until a natural dip in the landscape hid him from view.

"Jake, I will ride on," Silvano said. "Watch him and choose a good place for us to take him."

Sutter nodded. He knew the breed worked better on his own. Likely Silvano could take Brand by himself.

"Go ahead."

Reece watched the breed ride off. "So what do we do? Sit on our butts?"

"Hell no," Sutter grinned. "Nothing to stop us making our own play if the time suits."

Reece unlimbered his rifle and checked the action. "Tell you, Jake, that son of a bitch is going to be a hard one to kill."

"So everybody keeps saying." Sutter studied Reece's face. "You getting scared, Billy?"

"I just don't aim to get my fool head blown off. Not even to save Ben Wyatt's hide."

"So what are you goin' to do about it?"

Reece swung down off his horse. "*Do?* I'll tell you what I'm going to do, Jake. I'm going to get Brand before he decides to come after us."

Watching him climb the sandy slope that hid Brand from their sight Sutter shook his head. Reece was acting like a damn fool. Not that Sutter was about to stop him. Reece was a man grown and he'd been involved in enough gunplay to know the risks. Sutter let out an aggrieved sigh. He pulled his own rifle from the scabbard. If Billy Reece was about to start something it would be a wise move to be ready himself. Just in case there was any backlash.

★ ★ ★

Billy Reece heard Sutter moving somewhere behind him. He ignored the sound, concentrating on his own business. Above everything else he wanted a crack at Jason Brand. He'd heard a lot about the ex-US Marshal, and what he had heard told him that Brand was a tough hombre. Reece figured if he could take out someone of Brand's reputation it would boost his own. The thought felt good.

He reached the top of the slope and peered over. Brand and his prisoners were a distance away, but well within rifle shot. Reece bellied down and settled his long-barrelled Henry against his shoulder. He took his time, and when he touched the trigger the sound of the shot was loud in the stillness.

A jolt of excitement went through him as he saw Brand jerk in his saddle, then pitch to the ground. Reece let go a yell and scrambled to his feet.

"I got the son of a bitch!" he yelled.

He ran forward, over the crest of the slope. "C'mon, Jake, I done got the bastard for you!"

★ ★ ★

Brand lay for a moment, stunned by the fall. Even as he lay there, spitting dust out of his mouth, his senses were racing, pushing ahead, beyond the pain and the confusion of the moment. He knew he had to move and fast. Wyatt's bunch would be closing in. He could feel the burning stab of pain where the bullet had sliced across his left side, over the ribs. It had opened a ragged gash that was bleeding badly — but he knew it was more of an irritant wound than a fatal one.

He heard the rattle of hooves close by. Wyatt and Rimbaund were trying to spur their horses into movement. Brand turned his head, picking up the pair, and knew if he didn't get on his feet he might yet lose his prisoners.

Brand lurched upright, snatching his

Colt from its holster. He had dropped the shotgun when he'd left his saddle. Casting around he spotted it a couple of yards away and bent to scoop it up, biting back a gasp as pain from his side flared viciously. He looked back over his shoulder, in the direction the shot had come from. He saw Billy Reece running down the long, dusty slope. Reece had a rifle in his hands, and in the moment Brand located him Reece lifted the rifle and started shooting. Bullets kicked up gouts of dust around Brand, but Reece was firing wild, not giving himself time to locate his target.

Brand lifted the big Colt, dogging back the hammer. He picked up on Reece's moving figure, settled his aim and led Reece for a few yards before he eased back on the trigger. The big gun kicked against his palm as it slammed out its shot. He cocked and fired again.

Billy Reece appeared to pause in mid-stride. The Henry flew from his fingers, turning over and over before it struck the ground. A choking scream ripped from Reece's throat as the two .45 calibre bullets tore into him. The first took him in the chest, chewing a fist-sized hole as it blew out between his shoulders. The second bullet took away his throat in a scarlet burst of bloody flesh. Reece was flung to the ground, hitting his left shoulder. Bone snapped with a brittle sound and Reece slithered helplessly down the slope, coming to rest against a flat rock. He lay there, his body jerking in a series of weakening spasms until he died.

The moment he'd fired his two shots into Reece, Brand turned back to the jostling horses. Wyatt and Rimbaund were still struggling to gain control of the animals, hampered by the manacles they were wearing. Brand snatched up the reins of his own mount, jammed the Colt back in its holster and came up behind his prisoners with the shotgun barrels covering their backs.

"I were you I'd quit trying. You ain't

going anywhere. Not while I've got this scattergun on you."

Ben Wyatt swung round in his saddle, his face dark with rage.

"Don't bother to tell me," Brand said. "You're going to kill me if you get the chance — only you ain't going to get the chance."

He swung back in his own saddle. He had barely settled when he heard the whipcrack sound of a rifle. The bullet slashed the air to one side. A miss, but too close for comfort. Brand saw the lean figure of Jake Sutter on the high slope.

"*Move out!*" he yelled. "Let's go!" To add emphasis to his command he dropped the muzzle of the shotgun at the ground and touched one trigger. The boom of the shot spooked the horses and they took off at a dead run, Wyatt and Rimbaund doing their best to keep them close together.

Brand kept his own horse alongside as they thundered towards a stretch of rocky terrain. He wanted to put some tween himself and Wyatt's ... ey rode into the sprawl of ... flected heat of the sun hit ... dusty air was hot in their lungs. The shadows thrown by the mass of stone were heavy and black, lending the area a stark appearance.

Brand kept up the pace, refusing to ease off until they emerged from the rocks on the far side, plunging down a long, shale littered slope. Ahead of them now lay a wide, rugged spread of gullies and ravines and dry watercourses. The scant vegetation was the only touch of colour in the drab landscape.

As they sat their panting horses, taking a brief rest, Ben Wyatt raised his head.

"How long do you figure to keep this up?"

Brand glanced up from reloading his weapons. "Long as it takes," he said. "Most likely right up to the gates of Yuma Pen."

"Well it ain't over yet," Wyatt said defiantly. "You might have stopped

Billy Reece. Silvano and Jake won't be so damned easy."

"I'll be there to watch them put noose around your neck, Wyatt. You can count on that."

"Son of a bitch," Wyatt said bitterly. "I hope you die hard."

There was no reaction. Brand simply waggled the barrels of the shotgun. "Let's move out, boys."

They turned west again, Brand even more conscious of the pair still trailing him. Not that he could do anything about it right now.

Towards evening they found themselves riding alongside a narrow creek. The water was shallow but it was fresh. Brand called a halt to allow the horses to drink.

He eased himself in his saddle, taking the opportunity to survey the surrounding terrain. The survivors of Wyatt's bunch were out there, maybe close. He had heard of Silvano; the breed had a reputation as a loner, a self-sufficient individual who was reputed to be a master with any weapon he cared to pick up. 'Texas Jake' as Sutter was sometimes known was no beginner; it was rumoured that he had killed more than twenty men in gunfights; there was even a story about how Sutter had once braced Wyatt Earp himself outside the Long Branch; that incident didn't impress Brand too much — he had his own opinion about Earp and it wasn't all that complimentary. Despite his misgivings over tales that might have been little more than saloon gossip Brand did acknowledge the skills of Sutter and Silvano. A man was a fool if he underestimated his adversaries. On the other hand it didn't do to be overly impressed by dubious credits. Brand had faced men a lot tougher than either Silvano or Sutter, and *he* was still on his feet while they were viewing grass from the root end.

The moment the horses were rested and Brand had refilled their canteens, they rode on. Brand wanted them in a better place before full darkness. The day was slipping away fast, shadows deepening and the sky streaking crimson and pink, then flowing into a sombre purple.

He found what he was looking for in the last few minutes of light. A deep, natural basin, surrounded on three sides by high rock walls. There was only one way in or out, this being through a narrow defile that could easily be watched. Once inside Brand got Wyatt and Rimbaund off their horses and led them to a spot against one side of the basin.

"If you're thinking about trying anything — don't. I'll make it hard for you if you do," he told them coldly, leaving them in no doubt as to his meaning every word.

Keeping them both in sight Brand crossed over to where the horses stood. He loosened the cinches after he had tethered the animals. There was a sack behind his saddle. Freeing it Brand returned to where his prisoners sat watching him in sullen silence. Brand took a large piece of cooked beef wrapped in greased paper from the sack. Using his knife he cut thick slices and passed them to Wyatt and Rimbaund.

Rimbaund wolfed his down like a starving man. Wiping his mouth on his sleeve he took the mug of water Brand handed him.

"You building us up so we'll hang better?"

Brand's indifference to the question angered Rimbaund.

"Just what the hell are you getting out of this, Brand? You don't owe Adobe a damn thing. So why go through all this to get us to Yuma?"

"Cowboy, you really are as dumb as you look," Wyatt said. "Only reason why he's pinned on the badge is in his pocket. Money, you stupid ox. Go ahead, Brand, tell the hick the way it is."

Brand carried on eating. He knew Wyatt was simply trying to needle him. The outlaw would try any trick in the book to get Brand angry. To get him so damn mad he would . . .

"Rimbaund, you got horse shit for brains? Men like Brand, here, they need one thing to make them tick. Pay him enough he'd turn in his own grandmother." Wyatt was grinning now, his voice starting to grate on Brand's nerves. "He ain't nothing but a bounty hunter. Right, Brand?"

"You're telling it, Wyatt. Mind it's making me wonder how you got your reputation. Which was it, Wyatt? Your gun — or your mouth?"

A wild snarl rose in Wyatt's throat. He lunged up and forward, hurling himself bodily at Brand. His free hand clawed for Brand's throat. Rimbaund was dragged behind the raging outlaw, and he saw his own chance for freedom. As the three of them crashed to the ground Rimbaund tried to get his hand on Brand's holstered Colt. But he found that the handgun was pinned under Brand's body. The cowboy's attempt to snatch Brand's gun was curtailed when

Brand's fist smashed into Rimbaund's mouth. His head flew back, blood spraying from mashed lips. In the short time his head was drawn back Brand hit Rimbaund twice more. The final punch caught the cowboy in the throat, hard, and Rimbaund began to choke. He slumped back on his knees, losing interest in escape. Brand still had Wyatt to deal with. The outlaw's hand was clamped tightly around his throat, thick fingers biting into the flesh, with the whole of Wyatt's bodyweight crushing down on his arm. Brand found he was having problems getting the hand off his throat. Wyatt seemed possessed of superhuman strength as he squeezed, his face contorted with the effort. Brand fought back panic as his air was cut off. He realised he wasn't going to loosen Wyatt's grip unless he changed his tactics. He arched his body so he could get a grip on the butt of the gun Rimbaund had been so desperate to locate. He dragged the gun free, peering up at Wyatt through a red mist covering his eyes, and lashed out with the Colt's barrel. Right at that moment he didn't give a damn whether he killed Wyatt or not. The gun connected with a sodden crunch. Wyatt grunted in pain. Brand hit him again and again, and didn't stop until he felt Wyatt's fingers loosen their grip. Fresh air poured into his starved lungs. He twisted violently, shoving Wyatt's unresisting form off him, then rolled clear and staggered to his feet. The place where Billy Reece's bullet had clipped his side had started to bleed again. He could feel it soaking through his shirt.

Ben Wyatt lay slumped against the slope of the basin. He was staring up at Brand with wild eyes. Blood streaked his face, running freely from the gashes Brand's gun barrel had opened.

"You're going to have to kill me, Brand," he said hoarsely. "Because it's the only way you'll ever stop me."

Rimbaund was moaning softly to himself. He stirred and sat up, touching his hand to his bloody, crushed lips. He studied the wet blood all over his fingers.

"You bastard!" he yelled at Brand.

Brand put away his gun. He sat down and helped himself to a drink of water from the canteen. Splashed some over his face and throat.

"*Bastard!*" Rimbaund repeated.

Brand smiled. It was almost friendly. "Ain't I just!" he said.

11

THEY were up and in the saddle before dawn. By the time full light was spreading across the land the camp lay some three miles behind them.

Brand had hardly slept during the night. He had remained awake for most of it, watching his prisoners and keeping an eye out for any possible attack from Wyatt's partners. In the event nothing had happened, and Brand managed to snatch a little light sleep just before dawn, aware that the coming day might prove to be a long one.

The trip to Yuma was half over. Wyatt's partners would be determined to free him before Brand got too close to the prison town.

As the first blast from the risen sun caught them they were riding along a wide, sloping stretch of pale sand. It

164

rolled out ahead of them in smooth, undulating dunes, dotted here and there with rangy clumps of yellow grass. Brand knew they were leaving an obvious, clear trail but there was no point in trying to conceal their passing. Sutter, and especially Silvano, would know where they were at any given time, so Brand concentrated his attention on pushing forward.

Wyatt and Rimbaund, riding ahead of him, were maintaining a stoic silence now. Neither had spoken since struggling into their saddles. They were both nursing their wounds — mental as well as physical. It had hurt their collective pride failing to overpower Brand and break free. It had hurt just as painfully when they had received the punishment he'd handed out during the struggle. Rimbaund's lips were badly swollen, his throat bruised and sore. The bruises on Wyatt's face had swelled and discoloured, leaving it oddly misshapen. As far as Brand was concerned the silence was welcome.

The sand eventually gave way to another stretch of rock that presented a familiar pattern of ravines and gullies, snaking across the landscape to form a honeycomb of tortuous trails. Brand studied the rockbed, hoping to be able to find a way around. There was none. The tract of rock ran from north to south, seemingly endless. They pushed forward into the first ravine that seemed likely to offer a way through. It was narrow at first but rapidly opened out as they progressed along its course.

A long, slow half mile on the ravine abruptly opened onto a wide, deep basin. Brand drew rein and studied the way ahead. He wanted to keep moving in a westerly direction and was reluctant to be diverted. He found a rock-strewn gully, a long-ago riverbed. The course of the gully kept to a westerly direction. Brand, his rifle across his saddle, kept a keen eye on the crumbling rim of the gully as they moved along it. He was ever conscious of time slipping away.

Sutter and Silvano would have to make their move soon. Yuma drew closer with each step. And it was the waiting that had become the most difficult part of the whole venture. Brand found himself wishing the outlaws would make their play.

His eyes caught a momentary flash of sunlight on steel. It came from off to his left, yards ahead and above the rim of the gully.

He reacted instinctively. Snatching up the rifle resting across his thighs he fired one handed. His shot blended with one from the distant rifle. Brand felt a numbing blow to his left leg, well above the knee. The impact twisted him in the saddle, and Brand kept up the momentum by letting himself slip from the back of his horse. He broke his fall with his shoulder, tucking in his head and rolling in to the side of the gully. The hidden rifle fired a second time, the bullet kicking up a gout of dust inches from his left boot. Brand realised that as long as he stayed in the open he was fair game for the ambusher. He triggered a trio of quick shots at the distant location, then shoved to his feet. His wounded leg almost gave on him. Brand threw out his free hand to grab the closest stirrup of his riderless horse, leaning his weight against its side.

"Get off the damn horses and over to the side of the gully," he ordered Wyatt and Rimbaund.

"Hell, why should we?" Wyatt asked. "They ain't goin' to shoot at us if we sit here all day, Brand."

"They might not — but I sure as hell will," Brand said. "And you know by now I don't make idle promises."

They dismounted awkwardly, stumbling until they got the chain of the manacle sorted out.

"Over there," Brand ordered, pointing the way with his rifle.

They reached the far side of the gully, Brand using his own horse as cover until he was able to push against the overhang of the gully side. The man with the rifle was somewhere above him, unable to reach Brand with his weapon — but it was a stalemate because Brand couldn't reach the rifleman himself unless he moved out into the open again.

"Stay put," Brand snapped to Wyatt and Rimbaund. "First one tries anything stupid gets a bullet."

He heard the dry rattle of dislodged stones overhead. The rifleman was close, maybe directly above him. Brand swore silently, frustrated by his difficult position. All he needed was one quick shot.

"Yo . . . Wyatt!"

The voice was pitched low but the words reached them clearly.

Ben Wyatt smiled. A triumphant gleam filled his eyes.

"Here, Silvano! Waitin' and ready to go."

Brand didn't let Wyatt see it, but he was seething with anger at the outlaw's brazen act. Silvano, the breed, would have them pinpointed now.

169

A sharp stab of pain swelled in his leg. He sagged against the side of the gully, his hand clamped over the bleeding wound. The harshness of the pain told him the bullet was grating against bone. He fought back the nausea. There wasn't a thing he could do about it right now. Nobody was going to sit back and wait while he tended to his wounds.

Again he heard soft movement up on the rim of the gully. He wondered just what the breed was up to. He glanced at Wyatt and Rimbaund. *They* were watching him closely, debating, and just waiting for the moment they could rush him.

Brand shoved himself upright. Sweat trickled into his eyes and he shook his head to clear them. *Damn the breed!* Where the hell was he? Silence had blanketed the gully. The only sound he could hear was his own breathing.

He caught a glimpse of a dark shadow on the ground in front of him. It was the shadow cast by the rim of the gully. As Brand scanned the ragged outline he spotted movement. Only for a moment — but it was enough. He knew where Silvano was now. The breed was directly overhead, no doubt waiting for Brand to show himself. Brand watched the hunched shape for a while. Nothing happened. Silvano was a patient man. He could sit there for hours, not moving or making any sound.

So perhaps it was time to force the action!

Brand rattled some loose shale with his foot. Saw the shadow jerk to one side, then start to expand. He could picture Silvano moving forward, exposing himself beyond the protecting rim of the gully as he checked for sign.

As he gathered himself Brand caught a fleeting glimpse of Wyatt opening his mouth to call a warning to the breed.

Then he launched himself forward in a long dive that took him away from the protecting curve of the gully side, out into the open. He hit the ground and twisted over on to his back. The bright sunlight struck him in the face and he had to narrow his eyes against the glare. Despite that he could still make out the lean dark shape of the breed outlined starkly against the sky. Brand brought his rifle round, lifting the barrel and triggered three fast shots. There was an answering roar from Silvano's weapon, the bullet whacking the earth inches from his head.

And then Brand saw Silvano's body falling forward off the rim, twisting, turning. There was a bloody stain marking the front of the breed's shirt. Silvano hit the gully bottom, but instead of lying still he arched his wiry body and came to his feet, snarling in defiance. His rifle was still in his hands, the smoking muzzle seeking Brand. Silvano let go a wild, high yell as he saw him.

In that moment Brand himself reacted with the reflexes that had kept him alive for so long. As Silvano's rifle swung round to line up on him Brand began to trigger his own weapon, driving bullet after bullet into the breed's body. Silvano's mouth fell open, a ragged moan erupting from his lips as he was slammed back across the gully, ragged wounds appearing in his flesh under the impact of Brand's shots. His finger pulled back on the trigger of his own rifle, the weapon firing. Then Silvano's body arched stiffly and he crashed to the ground.

Brand hauled himself back to the cover of the gully side. He laid the rifle aside and pulled his Colt, easing back the hammer while he watched Silvano, convincing himself that the breed was dead this time.

It became very quiet. Even the horses had stopped milling about nervously. Powdersmoke drifted lazily in the shimmering air. Sunlight winked brightly on spent cartridge cases. The stench of burned powder mingled with the musk of spilled blood.

"Hey, Brand!"

Brand raised his head, sleeving sweat away. He stared at Wyatt.

"We've got a problem," the outlaw stated coldly.

Bart Rimbaund lay slumped against the side of the gully, his head tipped forward, eyes wide and staring. There was a large, wet patch of blood directly over his heart. Brand didn't need to ask. He knew Rimbaund was dead. He had taken the stray bullet from Silvano's rifle.

Brand fished the key to the manacles from his pocket and tossed it to Wyatt.

"Take it off Rimbaund and put it on your own wrist."

Wyatt did as he was told, finally holding up his chained wrists. "You feel safer now?"

"Always have."

Wyatt muttered under his breath. He threw the key back to Brand.

"Your trouble is you don't know when to quit, Brand."

"Been that way all my life. Family failing I guess."

Brand limped to where the horses stood. Shoving his rifle into the scabbard he hauled himself into the saddle, then led Wyatt's horse to where the outlaw sat waiting.

"Let's go."

Wyatt climbed to his feet and trailed to stand by the horse, making no effort to mount. Brand unlimbered the loaded shotgun and laid the muzzles on the outlaw.

"Don't play any more games, Wyatt, I'm feeling really shitty right at this time."

Wyatt climbed on board, picking up his reins. He scowled across at Brand.

"Don't give a man a chance do you?"

"With you around? Hell, no."

They moved on along the gully, leaving the dead breed to keep Rimbaund company. Two men who had allowed themselves to be ruled by violence — and eventually killed by it. Jason Brand couldn't help but wonder if it would be the way he would die.

There was no denying that he lived his life surrounded by violence. It was his trade. His profession — and the chance was that one day it would rear up and take him, answering the question that lurked at the back of his mind during every waking hour.

12

"LOOKS like you got one of 'em," Jake Sutter said. "Pity it wasn't Brand."

He was squatting on his heels in the gully, his gaze shifting from Silvano to Rimbaund and back. By the time the Texan had reached the gully it had all been done and over. Brand and Ben Wyatt were long gone, their trail leading out along the gully.

Sutter hadn't been surprised to find Silvano's body. He was developing a growing respect for the man called Brand. Anyone who could take Silvano couldn't be all bad. Sutter had always judged Silvano to be good — then again it didn't do to judge one man against another.

Sutter took a final look at Silvano. The breed had died hard. He had most probably died a surprised and disappointed man too. Yet the breed had said himself that Brand would be a hard man to deal with.

You were damn right about that, Silvano, he thought.

Sutter picked up Silvano's rifle. He also took the breed's gunbelt. They were no use to the dead man and extra firepower wasn't to be ignored. Sutter returned to his waiting horse. He hung the gunbelt from his saddlehorn, jamming the rifle in behind his blanket roll. Swinging into the saddle the tall Texan turned his horse along the gully.

Brand had a good lead on him. In this kind of country that could mean a lot. Sutter had no intention of pushing his horse too hard. The desertland that made up this section of the territory was no place to be on foot. If he did end up in such a predicament he wasn't going to be much use to himself or Ben Wyatt.

He pondered for a while on the thought that maybe he was being some kind of damn fool. Here he was, chasing across the country, risking his life trying to save a man from the gallows. He had the money from the Adobe bank raid in his saddlebags. Eleven thousand dollars. It was no fortune but it would do *one* man proud for a goodly time if he went careful. Some men might have said to hell with it and ridden the other way. But Jake Sutter, despite allowing the thought to fester for a while, was not other men. He and Ben Wyatt had ridden a lot of trails together. They had chosen their way of life and they had shared too many experiences. There was a bond between them that had come about simply through their sharing of those experiences. It was unspoken. Nevertheless it existed. Bound them in a way no chain ever could. They were men from the same mould. And they would never betray that unspoken trust. Sutter knew without ever asking that Ben Wyatt would have done the same for him if their positions had been reversed.

Sutter followed the gully to its natural end. It was noon now, with the sun high and brassy in the sky. He held his sweating horse on a crumbling slope, his hat pulled low to shield his eyes. Beyond his resting place the land slid away in a steep, undulating slope, and the tracks of two horses pointed the way west.

On the flatland he rode out across a wide salt flat. The crusted surface, white and crystaline, reflected the glare of the sun with blinding intensity. It hurt just to look at it. As he put his horse across the flat Sutter wondered if Brand had chosen this route deliberately — hard on himself and equally as hard on anyone following.

The dry, brittle surface of the salt crackled under his horse's hooves. The trail Sutter followed was clearly defined. He was grateful not having to stare too hard. The reflected glare of sunlight made his eyes ache. He let his horse make its own way. Allowed it to pick its own pace. The ride across the flats was slow and certain. Sutter relaxed in the saddle. He reached for his canteen and wet his lips. Took a small swallow. The water was warm but at least it was wet.

It took almost three hours to cross the salt flats. As they drifted away behind him, giving way to sandy, dry terrain, Sutter drew rein. He slid from the saddle. He was sweat-soaked. His skin and his clothes were crusted with salt. He sleeved it from his face, hearing the dry rasp of salt dropping away. Turning his attention to his weary horse Sutter spent some time cleaning crusted salt from around its eyes and nostrils. He gave it some of his precious water as well.

Leaving the animal to rest Sutter walked to the closest piece of high ground and scanned the terrain ahead. The desert rolled away before him, seemingly endless and eternally hostile. It would be like this most of the way to Yuma. It was a hard piece of country, with little to comfort a man for miles in every direction. Which had been one of the reasons why they had built Yuma Penitentiary out here.

He was about to turn back to his horse when he spotted two tiny specks moving slowly through the distant heat haze. They were miles ahead — but at least he knew he was on the right track. Sutter collected his horse and mounted up, taking up the trail once again.

"Hold on, Ben," he said softly. "I'm coming."

★ ★ ★

The salt flats lay far behind them, while the desert stretched in front of them. The horses moved with maddening slowness over the drifting, restless white sand. A faint wind had come up, lifting some of the sand in misty swirls. It got into their hair. Their eyes. Gritted up their clothing.

Brand hoped a sandstorm wasn't in the offing. That was all he needed. He had enough to contend with. The closer they got to Yuma, the more desperate would be Jake Sutter's need for some kind of violent act if he wanted to free Wyatt. Brand had spotted the Texan some time back. Sutter was well behind them. He was still coming though, and there was time for him to close the gap if he had a mind to. Brand considered Sutter the most dangerous. The man was no novice. He would put Brand to the test when he did make his move.

Brand was hoping he could reach Yuma before he fell off his horse. He'd managed to plug the hole in his leg with a kerchief, holding it in place with a strip torn from his shirt. The bleeding had finally stopped, but it could easily start again, and Brand had lost a fair deal before it had congealed. He could feel himself weakening, his strength ebbing with agonising slowness. He was occasionally overwhelmed by waves of nausea, which he had managed to conceal from Wyatt. It wouldn't last.

Sand, caught by a sudden gust of the rising wind, lashed at them. The wind *was* getting stronger. There *was* going to be a storm. Brand scanned the heavens. The thin white clouds were starting to drift. The distant horizon was dark with the heart of the storm and it was moving in their direction. The horses had picked up the scent of the freshening wind and what it promised, and they were becoming restless.

"Let's see you get out of this one," Wyatt said. He hadn't spoken for some time, and the sound of his voice was loud and harsh in Brand's ears.

"Don't worry," Brand said. "I never lost a prisoner yet. And you're especially important."

"Mister, I'm going to enjoy cutting out your goddamn heart!" Wyatt's face was dark with the rage brewing inside him.

The storm hit them at that moment. It came out of nowhere, with a muted howl, and it surrounded them in an instant. Sand was dashed in their faces, almost blinding them.

Brand lowered his head against the initial blast, hanging on grimly to his reins. He knew that these storms could last for days before blowing themselves out, or stop within a few hours. Until that happened, one way or the other, there was little a man could do apart from finding some kind of refuge. The alternative was to keep on moving. The trouble with that option was the ease by which a man could get himself hopelessly lost.

Brand chose to keep moving — mainly because he had little choice. Better to gain some distance, and hope he was getting closer to Yuma than to simply sit around and do nothing. He knew the risks he was taking. He was prepared to gamble. He knew the country well. Way back, long before he'd ever worn a badge, Brand had ridden scout for the Army. He had lived and fought and near died a few times out in this savage country. It was his land. He'd been born and raised in New Mexico. In terrain similar to this and he knew the land and its capricious whims. He could recognise when it was ready to seduce a man — and could tell when it switched to a killing mood. It wasn't an easy option living out here. A man didn't beat this land — he never mastered it. All he could hope for was to come to terms with it. No one, not even the Apache, subdued the land. All man did was to create a sense of toleration — living with the land, but never once trusting it.

Brand drew rein, reaching for a coil of rope hanging from his saddle.

"Now what?" Wyatt asked.

Brand knotted one end of the rope to the chains securing Wyatt's manacles. The other end went around his saddlehorn, snugged in tight.

"What the hell . . . ?" Wyatt demanded, spitting sand from his mouth.

Brand narrowed his eyes against the stinging sand. "I'm getting attached to you is all. I wouldn't want you drifting off and getting lost."

They moved on, the storm increasing in fury until the wind was almost dragging them from their saddles. Visibility had been reduced to a few yards.

Brand was starting to worry. Maybe his decision to keep moving had been wrong. The way things were developing they would have to hole up somewhere. The storm was growing too fast. And it was nowhere ready to peak yet. He hadn't anticipated its intensity. If they carried on travelling in this they would definitely end up lost and dead.

★ ★ ★

They came across the abandoned ranch by pure accident. Brand spotted the fallen fences first and realised they were close to some sort of habitation. He had no idea who it belonged to, or where it was located, but right now that didn't matter. If it offered shelter it would do. He let the horses follow the line of the fence and eventually they were able to make out the hazy shapes of buildings. As they moved closer Brand realised that the place was empty. Deserted. There was a long, low house. A barn with its big doors sagging and creaking on strained hinges. They crossed the yard, Brand turning the horses to the barn. Dismounting he and Wyatt led the animals inside. There was some feed in the stalls. Not the freshest but the horses were hungry enough not to be too concerned. Brand took his saddlebags and canteen. Tucking his rifle and shotgun under his arm, he motioned Wyatt in the direction of the house, following the outlaw across the storm-lashed yard.

Wyatt booted the door open and they stumbled inside. Shouldering the door shut Brand dropped the wooden bar in place, securing it. He dumped the saddlebags and canteen on the dusty tabletop. Crossing to a window Brand closed the shutters. Wyatt did the same with the others.

There was wood in a box beside the

open hearth. Brand fished a couple of matches from his pocket and handed them to Wyatt. The outlaw glared at him silently. Then he got down on his knees and began to build a fire.

Brand took a quick look round the room they were in. It was large, having been used as living room and kitchen. In one corner of the room a flight of wooden stairs led to the upper floor.

Flames began to flicker in the hearth as Wyatt got the small fire to grow. Luckily the wood in the box was tinder dry and flaking. It burned easily and the blaze grew quickly. Above the crackle of burning wood Brand could still hear the howl of the wind. It slapped against the walls of the house, rattling loose timber. The house had been well built and it resisted the battering storm.

"You got coffee in there?" Wyatt asked, indicating the saddlebags. He was on his heels before the fire. A big, heavyset man, his face dark with stubble and numerous cuts and bruises.

His flesh and his clothing were layered with pale dust. He fixed his red-rimmed eyes on Brand.

Brand handed over the sack of provisions he'd brought along. He also passed over his canteen.

"Go easy it's all we've got," he said.

"I still want some damn coffee," Wyatt grumbled.

Brand watched him make the coffee, hanging the pot from the hook that was suspended over the fire.

"This here storm is going to make Jake mad as hell," Wyatt said.

"He chose to wander around out there. Nobody invited him."

Wyatt fed more wood to the fire. "He's like me. Once he gets his teeth in he just don't seem able to let go."

"He keeps on coming he'll end up with something he never expected between his teeth," Brand said.

"Don't fret none," Wyatt said. "He'll come."

Brand grunted in frustration. "Can

we just drop the horseshit, Wyatt? Only thing that is certain sure is you ending up in Yuma. That why you're getting so anxious? Thinking maybe he won't get to you in time? The idea of being locked up in Yuma Pen starting to make you itch? I been told it's the place that sorts the men from the boys. You want to know something, Wyatt? I don't think you'll make it in there. Not now you're on your own. Kind of cuts you down to size I'd say."

Wyatt came up off the floor in a wild, unreasoning rush. His big hands, clasped together, sledged around and clubbed Brand across the side of the head, spinning him off balance. The metal band of one of the manacles tore a long gash down one cheek. Brand felt the blood stream down his face but didn't have time to worry about it. Wyatt cannoned into him, shoulder first and they stumbled together, crashing against the wall. Brand turned his hip in time to stop Wyatt's knee crushing into his groin. He caught the blow on his wounded thigh and the pain forced a strangled yell of pain from his lips. Reaction made him lash out, the knuckles of his hand scraping across Wyatt's mouth, pushing his head back. Blood flew in a hazy spray. Wyatt recovered surprisingly quickly, backhanding Brand across the face, then stepping in close to hammer both fists into Brand's stomach. The blow caught Brand unprepared, driving the wind from his lungs. As he sagged forward Wyatt hammered both fists down across the back of his neck. A roaring sound filled Brand's ears. He tasted blood in his mouth, and he was angry at himself for pushing Wyatt to the point where he had been forced to hit out. Brand sagged to the floor, then suddenly thrust upwards as Wyatt loomed above him. He caught Wyatt on the hip, knocking him away. Straightening up Brand saw Wyatt's boot swinging in at him. He moved aside to avoid it, then sank his fist deep in Wyatt's stomach, stopping the outlaw dead in his tracks. Brand let go with a roundhouse right that crushed Wyatt's lips against his teeth in a spatter of blood. Brand hit him again and again, forcing Wyatt back across the room. Wyatt faltered once and Brand slammed a powerful fist directly over his heart. Pain etched itself across Wyatt's bloody face. He swayed drunkenly. Brand delivered a left and a right to the jaw and Wyatt fell to his knees, head down, blood dripping to the floorboards. Brand hit him once more, a glancing blow with the toe of his boot that snapped Wyatt's head to one side. He rolled over on his back, panting for breath, making no attempt to move.

Brand crossed to his saddlebags. He pulled out a wrapped shirt and tore off a strip. He wet it from the canteen and used it to wipe his face. He leaned against the table, gripping the edge with his hands as waves of sickness welled up inside. He hurt all over and if he'd been allowed to admit the truth all he wanted to do was lie down and give in.

He forced himself to cross to the pot hanging over the flames. He filled a tin mug with scalding coffee and forced it down.

He made it to the door, freeing the bar and opened the door. The wind seeped in, bringing some coolness. It played over Brand's battered face as he stared out into the storm. The wind was still gusting across the yard, showing no sign of easing off.

He was about to close the door when the shot came. Brand saw the flicker of a gunflash, and then the bullet ripped a chunk out of the doorpost just above his head. A second shot followed, but by this time Brand had drawn back from the opening. He drew his Colt, easing back the hammer, fast realising that he wasn't going to have to wait any longer.

Jake Sutter had found him. And a showdown had to follow.

13

THE sound of the second shot had barely been whipped away by the wind when Brand hauled the door wide open and took an awkward dive out into the yard. He rolled to one side, coming up against the dried-out water trough, then held still, searching the swirling mist of dust. Sutter was out there and not far away judging by the stab of flame from his rifle.

It had been a split-second decision for Brand. He'd decided he would rather force the action and go after Sutter, rather than risk getting himself trapped inside the house. There was a showdown coming and Brand wanted it over and done with. Sooner that than a long, drawn-out seige.

He lay in the dust, his Colt thrust forward, cocked and ready. The storm was adding to his problems. It gave *him* cover but did the same for Jake Sutter. Brand was starting to get impatient. He needed something to happen. He was tired of being shot at, chased, and generally knocked about. This whole damned affair was sticking in his craw. He wanted it to be over. He thought fleetingly of the small, cool cell back in Adobe. Had he been a fool to let them talk him out of it? Letting them tempt him with money and a tin badge? He could have turned them down. At the time it had seemed an easy way out. The trouble had started the moment he'd accepted, becoming a target for too many guns, and too much violence . . .

He crawled forward, shielding his face with his left hand. Driven dust still peppered his flesh.

Sutter had fired from a spot some thirty feet from the house. There was no telling if he was still there. He could already be on the move, circling to close in on the house.

He made out the outline of the corral. Most of the fencing was down, the poles half buried in the drifting sand. Then Brand made out a large dark shape. It was a horse. *Sutter's!* It had to be the Texan's. Brand shoved to his feet, favouring his wounded leg. The horse didn't even lift its head when he neared it. Brand spotted something in the dust at his feet. A shiny cartridge case. There was another close by. Shells from Sutter's rifle.

So where was Sutter?

Instinct made him drop flat to the ground. The shot blasted through the swirling mist, passing above him. He caught a glimpse of the muzzle blast and snapped off a shot in return. Fired again a moment later. He heard a muffled grunt. The unseen rifle cracked a second time, the bullet burning its way along his back as Brand pushed to his feet. He returned fire again, moving forward. His pace was dictated by his leg. It was giving him more pain now. The buffeting wind slowed him too.

But his blood was up, surging hot in his veins. Nothing short of being dead would stop him now.

The shadow of a running figure, yards in front, prompted him to snap off a shot he knew had missed. He kept moving forward, wondering where Sutter was heading, and moments later he made out the dark bulk of the barn. Flattening himself against the front wall Brand flipped open the loading gate and ejected the spent cartridge cases. As he thumbed in fresh loads he conjured up a mental picture of the barn's interior. Stalls to the left of the doors. Feed-bins and shelves along the right. At the far end a tack-room. Running the length of the left side and across the rear wall was an upper level; a loft area for storing feed and sacks of grain. A fixed wooden ladder led up to the loft. The ladder was on the left, about halfway along the building's length.

Brand dogged back the hammer, set himself, and went in through the door.

He crouched, angling off to the right and moving into the shadows near the wall.

The blast of Sutter's rifle was loud in the confines of the barn. The bullet whacked the dirt floor inches from Brand. Three more shots followed, each one getting a little closer. The final bullet clipped the cloth of his shirt sleeve.

Hugging the side wall Brand pinpointed the spot where the shots had come from. Above him, from the loft section on the far side. Brand raised the Colt and triggered four rapid shots up through the loft flooring. The bullets ripped out jagged splinters of wood, raising dust in their wake. Following the shots came an abrupt rattle of sound. The thump of heavy boots. Stepping out from the shadows, into the centre of the barn floor Brand drove his final two shots through the loft floor. This time he heard a man swear. The voice was heavy with pain. Then silence. Brand waited, watching the loft, his fingers reloading the Colt with practised efficiency. His gaze never wavered. It was foolish to assume a man was out of action, or dead, if you hadn't actually got him in front of you.

Jake Sutter crawled into view at the top of the ladder. He slithered his body over the edge of the loft floor and started down the ladder. He lost his footing halfway down and fell, hunching up at the foot of the ladder. There was a jagged wound in his back, low down on the left side. It was bleeding freely. After a few moments Sutter lifted his head and stared at Brand. A wood splinter had torn open the left side of his face.

"Smart trick," Sutter said slowly. "I heard say you were good. They didn't tell you were tricky too. Don't ease the hurt none, but at least I got took by a professional, and not some backshooting pissant lookin' for a name."

Sutter climbed slowly upright, leaning against the loft ladder. He was holding his left hand against his body, trying to stem the flow of blood from the exit wound of one of Brand's bullets.

"Looks as if Ben is going to have to keep that appointment in Yuma after all," he said hoarsely. "What the hell, we had a good run, one way or another . . ."

As he spoke he dropped his right hand to the butt of his still-holstered handgun. The move was deliberate without being fast. He pulled the gun and angled it at Brand. Sutter was already a dead man and knew it, so he was choosing the quick way out. The hammer of his gun clicked back, and Brand put two bullets through his heart. Sutter arched over backwards, crashing heavily to the ground, his gun spinning from his fingers. He lay in a bloody, awkward sprawl on the barn floor.

Brand walked back out of the barn. He was halfway across the yard when he realised that the wind had already slackened off. The storm was weakening. The drifting dust had already thinned out. He could see the house clearly . . .

Wyatt!

He ran for the house, shouldering the door wide.

Ben Wyatt had struggled to his feet, his back to the door. He was reaching for the rifle Brand had left behind.

Brand didn't speak at first. He simply lifted the Colt and eased back the hammer. Wyatt heard the sound, his head lifting suddenly, fingers stroking the stock of the rifle.

"Jake?" he asked.

"Dead, Wyatt. Now get away from that rifle, or I'll give you the chance of meeting up with him here and now."

Wyatt turned slowly to face him.

"You'd gun down half the territory to make sure I won't miss my date with that hangrope."

Brand moved the rifle out of reach. "*Half* the territory, Wyatt?" He smiled thinly. "You *got* that many friends?"

Ben Wyatt's battered, bloody face

paled. The rage in his eyes was terrible to see and for a moment it looked like he might go for Brand, despite the loaded gun aimed at him. And then, just as quickly, he relaxed. Moving away from Brand he slumped wearily against the wall. He stared at Jason Brand, his expression bleak, and for the first time he made no attempt to conceal the dull gleam of defeat that showed in his eyes.

14

THEY reached Yuma just after dark. The storm, surprisingly shortlived, had completely blown itself out.

Brand trailed wearily along the main street and drew rein outside the jail. He took Ben Wyatt inside and told his story to the town's lawman. It took a lot of telling. The man in charge of Yuma's lawforce was a stolid, methodical man who didn't want to miss a single word. By the time Brand left the office, with Ben Wyatt already on his way to the grim prison overlooking the town, it was late. He located Yuma's doctor, and found a light on in the office. He spent an hour in the surgery, having the bullet removed from his leg, shedding blood and sweat in equal quantities. With the major work completed the doctor tended to Brand's other wounds.

Leaving the surgery Brand walked the horses to the nearest livery and had them tended to. After that he picked out Yuma's best hotel and tramped inside. The snotty young desk clerk wasn't having anything to do with the tall, washed-out saddletramp at first. He only saw the filthy clothes and the bloodstains. Brand was in no mood to argue. He showed the clerk his badge and the heavy Colt he was wearing and advised the kid to quit playing games. The registration book was shoved quickly under his nose. Brand signed it, took his key, and dragged himself upstairs to his room.

It turned out to be clean and comfortable. Brand dumped his weapons and saddlebags in a corner, peeled off his clothes and crawled beneath the covers.

He slept until late afternoon of the next day. He was roused by someone knocking on the door to ask if he needed anything. Brand ordered a meal and a bottle of good whisky. When it arrived he ate the food and downed half the bottle. The girl who had brought the food came back later and asked if she could do anything else for him. The look in her eyes suggested that certain of the services she was offering had nothing to do with the hotel. Brand said he needed a good hot bath and a shave, after which they might get together on a more personal basis. The girl, pretty and darkhaired, not only filled his bath for him, but turned out to have a steady hand when it came to shaving. Later she displayed her other talents, and Brand began a slow return to civilisation.

The girl's name was Jenny. Over the next week she learned as much as anyone ever did about the man named Jason Brand. He was pleasant enough but he held a great deal in reserve, unwilling to open himself up to Jenny. She decided it might not be a wise thing to dig too deeply. After all she was having a pleasant enough time. The hours spent in his room were by no means dull, and Jenny decided she could tolerate Brand's taciturn moods with little difficulty.

Brand soon began to feel restless. During the first few days he had completed the legal business concerning Ben Wyatt. After that the simpler pleasures, though diverting enough, began to lose their appeal. He was starting to look beyond Yuma. There wasn't much to hold him in the place. He had no desire to return to Adobe. Not just yet. He would be able to check on Judge Rice's condition by telegraph. The law in Yuma hadn't decided what to do about the inquest on the other killings back in Adobe. He had arranged with the law to get in contact with him when they needed his testimony. One day he might go back to Adobe. *Maybe*. Right now the town could handle its own affairs. He had fulfilled his deal with Adobe the moment he had handed Wyatt over to the Yuma authorities.

The girl, Jenny, was starting to

get that gleam in her eyes. Brand recognised it straight off. It was the time when a casual affair stopped being casual. When that happened he felt the need to move on.

He breakfasted, on the morning of the day he had decided to ride out, in the hotel dining room. Later he would see Jenny and tell her he was leaving. Then he could settle his bill and go. His mind was occupied with such thoughts as he returned to his room, opening the door and stepping inside before he realised he had locked it earlier.

"Come in, Brand. After all it is your room."

Brand closed the door. His right hand was curled close to the butt of his Colt while he inspected the man standing at the window. Tall, broad-shouldered and dressed in a dark suit, with a white shirt. His boots were highly polished. Brand judged him to be in his mid-forties. His thick hair was silver-grey, the face brown and the eyes steady and keenly alert.

"Should I know you?" Brand asked. He was curious now that he had decided the man presented no threat.

"No. On the other hand I know all about you, Mister Jason Brand."

"It appears you have the advantage."

The other smiled. "The name's McCord. Frank McCord."

The name didn't mean a thing to Brand. He tossed his hat on the bed and crossed over to the wardrobe to start packing his gear.

"All right, Mister McCord, spit it out."

"You've taken some finding," McCord said. "I missed you after the Dorsey affair. Didn't pick up your trail until a few days back. From what I hear Adobe will never be the same again."

"I guess all this is leading up to something?" Brand faced McCord. "I'm leaving Yuma today, so quit fiddle-footing and tell me what's on your mind."

"I've got a job for you, Brand."

"I didn't figure you were trading beaver pelts. Right now I don't feel like taking anything on. Look me up in a month or so and maybe we can talk."

McCord reached into his coat and took out a small leather folder. He opened it and held it out for Brand to see. Pinned inside the folder was a gold and blue badge in the shape of a shield. Engraved on the shield were the words — *Justice Department-Special Agent.*

"Very nice," Brand said. "I never heard of you."

"No reason you should," McCord said. He put the badge away. "Outside of Washington we don't exist. All our people work undercover and on their own."

"How do I come into this?

"I want you to join us."

Brand smiled mirthlessly. "If you know all about me you'll know I was thrown out of the US Marshals office."

"I know about that, Brand. It doesn't

concern me. We choose people by our own selection process. If a man fits our needs we go for him and forget the past. And you fill our needs, Brand. Hell, man, you're too good a lawman to waste your time playing bounty hunter. There's a place for you in my department, and believe me you'll get all the damned action you want. Out in the field you run things your way as long as you get results. I'll yell bloody murder if I think you've gone too far. But I'll expect you to give your best every minute of the day and night. And you had better, mister, because you will be paid well for doing it."

"Do I get a chance to think about it?" Brand asked.

He was interested — but wary. He had no intention of becoming tied up with another outfit that might turn on him one day and throw him out into the cold. It had happened once to him and the experience still left a bitter taste in his mouth.

"If you're worrying about getting

kicked in the teeth again — don't," McCord said. "I don't work that way. The assignments we handle are the kind that call for direct, tough solutions and we go out expecting trouble. There won't be anyone around to start shouting if you have to play dirty."

The offer was becoming more appealing with every passing moment. It was hard to resist. It was, after all, the sort of work that drew Brand like a moth to a flame. He was being tempted.

"Who would I be responsible to?"

"Me as head of the department. There is just one more man. The ultimate authority."

McCord handed Brand a folded sheet of thick paper. Brand read what was written on the paper — it was the very same offer McCord had made to him.

"The man would like to meet you," McCord added.

Brand ran his gaze down the letter,

reaching the signature at the bottom. The signature and the official seal of the *President of the United States*.

"Makes it kind of hard for a man to refuse," Brand said.

"Are you going to?" McCord asked.

"I haven't decided yet," Brand answered.

Even as he spoke he knew what his answer would be. What it had to be. In his mind he *had* decided, making his choice and committing himself to walking the only road that lay open to a man such as himself . . .

The end of HARDCASE . . . but Jason Brand will be back in LOBO . . . out on his first assignment for Frank McCord and the Justice Department.

FIGHTING RAMROD
Charles N. Heckelmann

Most men would have cut their losses, but Frazer counted the bullets in his guns and said he'd soak the range in blood before he'd give up another inch of what was his.

LONE GUN
Eric Allen

Smoke Blackbird had been away too long. The Lequires had seized the Blackbird farm, forcing the Indians and settlers off, and no one seemed willing to fight! He had to fight alone.

THE THIRD RIDER
Barry Cord

Mel Rawlins wasn't going to let anything stand in his way. His father was murdered, his two brothers gone. Now Mel rode for vengeance.

ARIZONA DRIFTERS
W. C. Tuttle

When drifting Dutton and Lonnie Steelman decide to become partners they find that they have a common enemy in the formidable Thurston brothers.

TOMBSTONE
Matt Braun

Wells Fargo paid Luke Starbuck to outgun the silver-thieving stagecoach gang at Tombstone. Before long Luke can see the only thing bearing fruit in this eldorado will be the gallows tree.

HIGH BORDER RIDERS
Lee Floren

Buckshot McKee and Tortilla Joe cut the trail of a border tough who was running Mexican beef into Texas. They stopped the smuggler in his tracks.

BRETT RANDALL, GAMBLER
E. B. Mann

Larry Day had the choice of running away from the law or of assuming a dead man's place. No matter what he decided he was bound to end up dead.

THE GUNSHARP
William R. Cox

The Eggerleys weren't very smart. They trained their sights on Will Carney and Arizona's biggest blood bath began.

THE DEPUTY OF SAN RIANO
Lawrence A. Keating and Al. P. Nelson

When a man fell dead from his horse, Ed Grant was spotted riding away from the scene. The deputy sheriff rode out after him and came up against everything from gunfire to dynamite.

FARGO: MASSACRE RIVER
John Benteen

The ambushers up ahead had now blocked the road. Fargo's convoy was a jumble, a perfect target for the insurgents' weapons!

SUNDANCE: DEATH IN THE LAVA
John Benteen

The Modoc's captured the wagon train and its cargo of gold. But now the halfbreed they called Sundance was going after it . . .

HARSH RECKONING
Phil Ketchum

Five years of keeping himself alive in a brutal prison had made Brand tough and careless about who he gunned down . . .